Seasons of Love

A Kindred Hearts Novel

TaKisha Trenean

Forever humbled, forever grateful. To the friends who listened as I worked through my storylines and gave input to put my brain back on track. To those who instilled confidence with their feedback and excitement. To my fellow female authors who inspired and made this dream believable just by following theirs. To those who supported in any way. Thank you.

Contents

Prologue

Zolee sat her cup down and sashayed her way towards the front door. She looked back at Cooper and asked if he was coming. He chugged the rest of his drink and followed. Her fat ass and curvy hips baited him and led him out of the door. While they patiently waited for the elevator, Cooper's watchful eye studied Zolee. Her arms were crossed and she twisted her body from side to side while watching the numbers above the elevator door.

"Yo, you good?" Zolee jumped but it was barely noticeable. She licked her lips and wiped the palms of her hand on her butt.

"Yeah. Yeah, I'm good. I'm great." Cooper could tell that she was nervous and he wanted to get her out of her head. The door opened and he allowed her to step in first. Before the elevator door could close, he had Zolee pent against the back wall. He brushed his lips down her neck then kissed the sensitive spot between her chin and collar bone. His lips curled up in a smile when he felt her body shiver then relax and lean into him. Unable to help herself Zolee dipped her head down and back up until their lips connected. As Cooper's hand inched up her thigh, the elevator came to a stop and chimed. Cooper groaned in displeasure. He pulled back but couldn't stop staring at Zolee. She was a whole other type of beauty. It was understated but her key features could make others envious. Her sexy dark eyes just drew him in.

"You are so fuckin' beautiful." He kissed her one more time, then used his hand to stop the door from closing. "Lead the way."

As Zolee made her way to her apartment with Cooper's hand placed at the small of her back, she was astounded by how relaxed but excited she was. She almost chickened out while waiting on the elevator but Cooper's unexpected kissed erased any doubt that she had. Normally, Zolee would have freaked out about inviting a complete stranger into her home with the promise of one night of passion in her bed, her safe place and personal sanctuary. She moved into the midtown high rise after her breakup with Lorenz. No man had been in her bedroom, let alone her apartment but for some reason she wanted this man in her space; she craved his energy. This disarmingly handsome man who seemed to understand her disdain for this day and normalized it. This man who looked at her like he wanted to taste every inch of her. This man whose smile was going to be the death of her. Everything within her told her that tonight, he would ruin her for any man; nothing would be the same after.

Cooper's initial plan was to pounce on her the minute the door closed, but something was telling him that he needed to take his time and make this moment unforgettable for Zolee. The air around them shifted and Zolee felt trapped under Cooper's gaze. He caressed her face and ran his hands through her locs. When their lips connected, Zolee's legs almost gave out from under her, but Cooper's strong arms held her up.

"Mmm Coop," Zolee whispered. Slowly, they took their time relieving each other of their clothes. They both took a moment to take each other in. Zolee smirked at Cooper's impressive body. With a sexy six-pack, broad back and strong thighs, he was thick and almost all muscle, but not too muscular. She'd never seen a body like that live and in color and in her apartment. Zolee's eyes landed on his erection and they nearly popped out of her head. He was the trifecta; handsome, fine, and was well, very well endowed. If he knew how to use it then he was officially a damn unicorn. Cooper smirked at her reaction and made it jump which made Zolee roll her eyes. Coop committed Zolee's body to memory from her full, perky breast, down to her modest hips and perfect ass.

Zolee looked towards the floor under Coop' scrutiny, but he tilted her head up by her chin.

"Don't do that. You don't look like the type to be modest or embarrassed. I know that you know you look good."

Zolee giggled then pushed a stray loc out of her face. "It's you, you're making me feel things that I..." She shook her head and kept her admission to herself.

"Never mind, it's stupid." Zolee started to ramble but Cooper shut her up by sticking his tongue in her mouth. They kissed with such passion, like two lovers who'd known each other longer than a few hours. Cooper's hands grazed the side of Zolee's ribs, making her shutter; she hadn't been touched in so long, not since Lo. Her heart rate quickened when his hands finally made their way to her center. He groaned and bricked up even more when he discovered how wet she was. Zolee wrapped her arms around his neck and shamelessly grinded into his finger, which he wasted no time inserting into her. With two fingers inside of her and his thumb pressed into her clit, he worked Zolee to her first orgasm. When her head flung back from the onslaught of pleasure, he took the opportunity to kiss, lick and suck on her neck. Cooper held her tight as she trembled in his arms.

"Ahh Coop. Fuck. Mmm." With her still panting from the orgasm, Cooper backed her into the nearest wall and kneeled down in front of her. He tapped her thigh twice.

"Put your foot on my shoulder." Zolee quickly obliged and Cooper dove right in inhaling her scent. He latched onto her clit and sucked until it stiffened. Cooper ate Zolee's kitten like it was the best thing he ever tasted. The feel of his tongue in addition to slurping sounds he created made Zolee hold the back of his head and roll her pelvis into his face. That only turned Coop on even more and made him go even harder. He licked her from the top to her ass and swirled his tongue in quick circles.

"Yes, just like that. Ahhh Coop. Wait Coop. I-I'm cu-cumming again. Shit, I'm cumming."

"That's right baby don't hold that shit in. Fuck you taste so damn good." With that Zolee bucked against his face as he gripped her ass and continued to feast on her until her orgasm subsided. He made sure to lick both her thighs and her throbbing core, not leaving a single trace of her powerful release. Zolee could barely stand, so he picked her up and wrapped her legs around him; he held her up by her ass.

"Which door to the bedroom?"

"Down the hall, second door." Zolee planted soft kisses on his neck and face. Cooper made his way to the bedroom and deposited Zolee on the bed. She sat up and attempted to pull him closer so that she could take him into her mouth. Cooper step back and shook his head.

"You don't have to do that Zolee. I want this night to be about… Ahh shit! Damn baby." Before Cooper could complete his sentence, Zolee took him into her mouth and nearly swallowed him whole. The warmth and wetness of her mouth made his toes curl. He entangled his hands in her hair and guided her movements, but she honestly didn't need any help. She used her tongue to tease and taste the underside of his penis, then the tip. Zolee gripped the base and her head bobbed up and down. The mixture of her movements and her saliva created a sound that drove Cooper wild. He had to clamp down on his back teeth to stop from moaning out loud like a bitch. When Zolee pulled back and sucked him at the same time while massaging his balls, a moan escaped from his mouth.

"Argh, shit girl. Wait, hold up." Cooper didn't want to cum in her mouth but needed to be balls deep inside of her.

"Lay back on the bed." Cooper looked around for his jeans and remembered that they were in the living room. He told Zolee that he'd be back and jogged to grab the condom out of his wallet. He cursed himself for only having one. Re-entering the room, he was quick to sheath himself while his eyes rove over Zolee's naked body. She looked perfect with her locs tossed over her shoulder and her eyes half masked.

Zolee sat up when she noticed Cooper was back in the room; she felt his presence. Instinctually she opened her legs for him. She felt flutters in the pit of her stomach as she anticipated the next round of this unexpected night. Her breathing increased and her chest visibly rose up and down. Cooper continued to lustfully study her body which made her grow impatient.

"Coop please." She whined and tossed her head back. Before she could bring her face back down to look at him, he'd crawled on the bed and settled between her legs. He hooked his arms around her legs and slowly began to push his hardness into her. Zolee winced at the intrusion but because she was so wet Cooper had no problem gliding into her slick center. Cooper cursed under his breath as Zolee's warm, tight pussy gripped him and pulled him in deeper. He'd never experienced anything like it. He began moving in and out of Zolee. He tried to keep his eyes open and enjoy her expressions of ecstasy but every time he pulled back his eyes fluttered closed.

"Fuck Zo. You feel so damn good." Zolee smiled and moved with him; she kept up with his rhythm as they moved in sync with each other. Zolee's movements quickened and she rolled her hips and pushed against his pelvis. Her stomached fluttered again as wave after waves of pleasure washed over Zolee's body. It hit her so hard she couldn't form a sound at first then finally a scream escaped out of her mouth. Her pussy contracted around Cooper's dick, almost causing him to bust prematurely so he pulled out until she finished. He leaned down and licked her vulva before kissing her clit.

"Ah, ah, ah. Oh my god, oh my god." With her eyes still closed Zolee smiled and sighed with satisfaction.

"Mmm. Cooper?"

"What's up Zo?"

"Lay on your back." Cooper rolled on his back and Zolee straddled him. She used her tongue to trace around his six-pack and kissed a trail up to his lips. Cooper clasped the back of her head and eased his tongue into her mouth as their lips smashed together. Their tongues danced around each other. Zolee eased down onto Cooper's slick erection, which felt rock hard. Cooper gripped her thigh with his free hand. Zolee rocked slowly until she adjusted to his size and being on top. Zolee began to bounce up and down on Cooper; the fact that she was in control turned her on as she coated Cooper with her essence. Based on Cooper's breathing she knew he wasn't going to last much longer. As she rode him, she placed her hands on his knees and leaned back as she rolled her hips up and down and side to side. Her head fell back as he began to hit her g-spot, sending what could only be described as electrical currents up and through her body. Sweat ran down her back and mixed with Cooper's. Cooper gripped her hips to anchor her and began to slam her up and down his pole. Zolee cried out from both pain and pleasure.

"Shit Cooper. You're so fucking deep. Shit, shit!"

Cooper growled as he felt himself coming undone. "That's right Zo cum all over this dick."

Zolee felt the flutters again, then the feeling as if there was a spring in her canal that was being held down. When the spring popped, tears sprang from her eyes and she squirted all over Cooper, who moaned and growled through his own release. She collapsed on top of him and both of them inhaled and exhaled liked they'd just finished running a marathon. Cooper held Zolee tight, both of their skin glowed because of the sheen of sweat from their love making.

"Zo, you are fucking amazing. You know that?" Cooper's words touched Zolee who lazily grazed her fingers down his side.

"No, that was all you. I've never come like that before, like I've never squirted. That was... shit."

"Guess ol' boy wasn't puttin' it down in the bedroom like ol' Coop here." Zolee rolled her eyes and smirked.

"I thought I picked up on some arrogance earlier. Come on let's wash up because I am tired."

They washed up in the shower together then changed the sheets on the bed. To Zolee's surprise, Cooper slid under the covers instead of getting dressed and leaving.

"What? Am I on your side?" Zolee slowly shook her head no.

"Well bring your ass on." Zolee rolled her eyes and joined Cooper in the bed.

"I was trying to be nice, but you are on my side."

"Well this is the side that I sleep on in my bed."

"But this ain't your bed. It's mine." Cooper grabbed Zolee then pulled her on top of him and held her tight.

"Now we both get what we want." Zolee snickered and laughed when he tickled her face with the stubble of his five o'clock shadow. Zolee felt her eyes grow heavy as she fought to stay awake because she didn't want the night to end.

"Coop?" she mumbled into his chest.

"What's up Zo?"

"Happy Birthday and thank you."

"No, thank you."

Before dawn broke and the sun began to color the sky, Coop tip toed out of the bedroom and dressed in the living room while Zolee remained asleep. If he didn't get back to his hotel room and pack, he was going to be late for his flight. He called Ashli, whom he had five missed calls from.

"Dude get out of my friend's pussy and get your ass here!"

"Watch your damn mouth Ash. I'm on my way now."

"Sooo."

"So what?"

"Was it the best birthday like I promised?"

Cooper couldn't help but smile as the memories of the night before and early morning flashed in his head.

"It was. Thank you."

"You're welcome and don't make me regret introducing you to ZoZo. She'd special Coop." Cooper nodded in agreement as if she could see him.

"I've come to see that in the short period of time I've spent with her. I'll see you when I get there."

"Hurry nigga!" Cooper hung up the phone without a response. He took a minute to look towards Zolee's room before he headed out to catch his flight to Greece.

When Zolee woke up the next morning she was groggy and slightly hung over from the shots mixed with the wine she drank, or she was hungover from Cooper. Cooper! Zolee shot up in her bed and looked around her room. She gasped and her mouth fell open; she covered her mouth with her hand.

"Oh Coop!" Zolee's room was filled with bouquets of purple and white helium balloons and several floral arrangements of purple lilies. Next to her was an assortment of truffles, a card, and a small box. Zolee opened the small gift box with zest. Inside were three flawless diamond bangles. With the back of her hand Zolee wiped the tears from her eyes and sniffled. Her lips curved upward into an amused smile and she laughed as she read the card that included his number.

Zo,

First holiday in the books! Following your father's tradition diamonds for a diamond. One for each year you didn't get your Valentine. Thank you for making this one of my best birthdays ever. #epic See you next holiday. Happy Valentine's Day.

Xoxo Coop

For the first time in a long time Zolee was looking forward to the year ahead of her. She had no clue what was in store for her but she felt confident that she was ready to take the journey to get back to becoming the Zolee everyone knew and loved. She wasn't going to be the exact same person because losing her dad had definitely changed her, but she was ready to get out of the pit she'd been in and live. On top of that Zolee was more than happy to include Coop on this journey. For the first time in three years she couldn't wait for the next big holiday.

Winter

Chapter 1

Knowing that she only had about another hour to spare, Zolee quickly ate her dinner and declined dessert, in spite of the insistence of her date. Harry was tall, caramel complexion and bald, but it fit him. He always smelled good and had the sweetest smile. They'd met during a photo shoot. Harry's family owned a successful real estate company and had hired her to do their annual photos, which included group and individual shots. Harry chatted her up the entire time and turned up the charm whenever he was in front of her camera. He was funny, smart, and had a great personality. While she was packing up he asked for her number and assisted with taking her equipment to her car. He was the perfect gentleman and extremely, pretty. Hell he was prettier than her. Zolee's eyes wandered over Harry. He was immaculately dressed in a suit that was flawlessly tailored to fit his slim frame. Zolee sometimes questioned what the hell he saw in her. He was expensive wine and caviar and she was cheap wine and pizza. They'd been dating for almost a month now but hadn't made things official and it was not due to his lack of trying. Zolee just wasn't one hundred percent sold on him. He was great in bed but there were no sparks, no fireworks, no butterflies. Harry didn't make her feel like... Dammit. Zolee shook away the thought as her body visibly shivered.

"Hey, are you cold?" Harry leaned forward and started to remove his jacket. From the moment he first laid eyes on Zolee his plan was to make her his. In his eyes she was beautiful; the type of woman any man would want on their arm. Her strong yet warm personality drew him in and she made a lasting impression on him. If she hadn't given him her number that day he would have done whatever he needed to do to see her again.

"No! No I'm fine, just a case of the chills." Zolee cleared her throat and wiped her mouth with the napkin. "You ready to go?"

Harry smirked as his eyes grew heavy, laced with desire. He couldn't wait for the next opportunity to sample the pure gold that was between Zolee's beautiful, strong chocolate legs. Zolee was about four years older than him. Harry loved the fact that she was comfortable with both her body and her sexuality. She was nothing like the women his age who only wanted to have sex with the light off. Zolee didn't care as long as she got hers and that only challenged Harry to tie her down.

"Of course beautiful. Let's go." Harry paid the tab and left a generous tip on the table before he held his hand out to help Zolee out of her seat. Zolee smiled and followed him out of the door. As they drove back to her apartment Zolee's phone continued to vibrate but she did her best to ignore it. Zolee's leg shook as she checked the time on her watch several times. Harry looked over at her and his forehead creased.

"Everything alright over there?"

"Huh? Yeah. Sure. It's just this show that I've been dying to catch comes on tonight."

"I thought you wasn't big on TV."

"No, I'm more of a movie person, but it's all my friends talk about so..." Zolee released a sigh of relief when they reached her condo in record time. Lucky for her Harry was known to drive well above the speed limit. When he hit the blinkers to turn in the parking garage, Zolee stopped him then gave him a weak smile.

"Um can you drop me off at the front? Me and the girls had plans to watch the show together." Unable to hide his disappointment, Harry's shoulders slumped but he quickly recovered.

"Yeah, sure, I need to wrap up some paperwork anyway, but you owe me Lee." Zolee cringed at his chosen nickname for her. It was exactly how her asshole of an ex-boyfriend used to refer to her. Harry put the car in park when he pulled up to the building. Zolee's exotic scent was driving him wild. He leaned in for a kiss which Zolee accepted. Harry was an okay kisser but it was all about him and the more he got into it the sloppier his kisses were. He might as well been kissing himself in a mirror. She felt like an outsider so she pulled away before he swallowed her whole and gave Harry a meek smile. She traced her lips with her fingers.

"Thank you for tonight. As usual you were the perfect gentleman."

"And you were the perfect companion." Zolee paused before getting out of the car. *Companion?* That was it. That was why she couldn't fully connect with Harry. She sometimes felt like an accessory when she was with him, like an afterthought.

"Bye Harry."

Zolee jogged inside the building and took the elevator up to her floor. She danced with her legs held tightly together as she shifted from one foot to the other. Hopping off the elevator, Zolee sprinted down the hall. When the door opened to her apartment Zolee nearly fell in and she swung the door in hopes that it would close since she had an automatic lock. She made a mad dash to the bathroom, lifted up her dress, pulled down her panties and plopped down on the toilet. She exhaled and sighed in relief as her bladder expelled the warm liquid she'd been holding on to for the last thirty minutes.

"Shit! Thank you Jesus!"

After she flushed the toilet, Zolee washed her hands just in time to hear her phone ring. She had an incoming FaceTime call. Unable to contain the smile on her face she quickly swiped to answer the call.

"What up Zo?" His deep raspy voice echoed in the bathroom as she turned off the lights and fell into the royal purple accent chair in her reading nook.

Zolee sighed. "Coop..." He was wearing a dark blue Henley with a skully on his head. He was currently in New York City. His huge smile warmed Zolee up. He was never too cool to flash those perfect set of teeth.

"What's up baby! Happy St. Patrick's Day!"

"Are you serious? Boy bye! We agreed on *major* holidays." Zolee rolled her eyes and crossed her short legs. She wiggled her toes and examined her purple painted nails. Cooper shrugged.

"I'm just fuckin' with you." Cooper took in Zolee's appearance. She was wearing a full face of makeup and looked like she was wearing a dress, her breast almost spilled out of the top half. Her eyes were seductively low like she'd had a couple glasses of wine. He smiled. "Damn, you look good. How've you been?"

Zolee blushed and ran her hand over her wild locs.

"Good. Just getting in from a... Well a..."

"A date Zo?" His eyebrow lifted and Zolee could have sworn she saw a hint of annoyance flash before his eyes.

"Yeah sort of." Zolee shook her head, her cotton soft hair bounced around. She was flustered. Cooper smirked.

"It's cool Zo." *It really wasn't.* After the night they shared on Valentine's Day, Cooper secretly felt like Zolee was his. His feelings for her were primal and he hated the thought of another man being around her; he'd become territorial in a short period of time. He wanted to break this dude's face. He knew that he was fucked up for feeling that way being that he was still sexing his ex and back and forth with cutting her off completely, but Zolee was his. A part of her would always be his.

"Is it the same clown from before?" Well there went playing it cool. Zolee gave him a pointed look before she tossed her head back and laughed.

"He is not a clown Coop. Harry is a really nice guy, like you."

"ZoZo baby I am far from being a nice guy." Zolee bit her lip then ran her hands through her hair again. Her wrist adorned the bracelets Coop gifted her and they song a melody whenever she moved. Cooper wanted nothing more than to give Zolee exactly what she needed because there was no way they would be talking right now if *Harry* was handling her right.

"So what's the next holiday? The Fourth?"

Zolee shook her head no. "Gosh Coop I can't wait that long. What about Easter?" Zolee couldn't help but admit that she was excited for the next time that she got to see Coop in the flesh. Her body hummed with need every time they talked. She couldn't wait to be locked inside her home with him.

"The fuck Zo? Ain't that like a religious holiday?"

"Yeah I guess. Well we don't have to do anything…"

"Nah. I'll come early and leave that Wednesday after." Cooper looked down at his phone and saw that his ex was calling. He didn't want to answer but he knew she wouldn't stop until he did.

"Yo I need to take this call."

"Oh, okay. Cool." Zolee's mood deflated from disappointment and Cooper instantly felt like shit.

"Tomorrow?"

"Always." Zolee and Cooper ended their calls like they always did, but Zolee was uneasy about it this time. They'd agreed that when they were talking it was their time together, no interruptions. She wondered who was important enough for him to cut their conversation short. As Zolee wrecked her brain at the possibilities, she stripped down to nothing and headed back to the bathroom to shower. She had a long day ahead of her tomorrow and needed proper rest.

"Yes! Oh, my God that is it right there. You. Are. Gorgeous. That ain't nothing but black girl magic!"

Zolee snapped shot after shot as Beyoncé played from the speakers. The up and coming blogger blushed as she posed. Today's shoot was at the botanical gardens, a beautiful location full of lush foliage and exotic flowers. She was a little timid at first, but eventually warmed up. She found Zolee likeable and easy to get along with.

"You are going to love these Keesha. The camera absolutely loves you! I think I got enough." Zolee placed her camera back on the tripod and went to her laptop to view the photos.

"Thank you Zolee for making this so easy and fun! I'm so glad that I found your Instagram page. I can't wait to see the finished product."

"I think you're going to love them." Zolee smiled then waved Keesha over to the computer. She clicked through a few pictures to give Keesha a preview of her photos.

"Oh my God! These are... I can't believe that is me!" Keesha fanned her face as she teared up. Zolee stood up straight and pulled her into a hug.

"Aww. You are beautiful girl! Me and my team just enhanced it. I am going to work on editing these and should have these back to you for review in a week."

"Thank you! I'll talk to you in a week!"

"Take care!"

Zolee and her team began to pack up the props and back drops. She could not wait to get her own studio instead of renting spaces. She was working hard working several jobs to save up the money for her perfect space. Zolee worked with an independent team that included a hairstylist, makeup artist and an assistant who worked for free while she was in school. She wanted the experience and was willing to do it at no cost to Zolee. Yara had been following Zolee on social media for years and was just excited to work with her. Together they packed everything up into their two cars.

"I know I say this all the time but I appreciate you so much Yara."

"Don't mention it Zo. I'm glad to get the work experience." Yara waved Zolee off and flashed her innocent smile.

"I'm going to start paying you one day soon. I owe you." Yara attended the local university and was majoring in business and communications. She wanted to own her own PR firm one day. Once the two had everything back into the storage unit, Zolee treated Yara to lunch then headed back home. When She finally checked her phone she had missed calls from her mom, Harry, and Ari. She decided to call Ari back first.

"ZoZo!"

"What up? What's going on?"

"Oh nothing... Just calling to check on my girl. Are you free to hang?"

"Um yeah, let me wash up and change clothes then I'll come over."

"I'm hungry Zo I want to go out." Zolee paused in the middle of kicking off her socks. After all these years she still didn't know how her friend did it. Ari was a therapist and ran her own practice with employees but was also the posterchild for work-life balance. She practiced what she preached. With the help of her trusty planner she planned her whole life out both professional and personal.

"You are lucky that I love you and that I'm hungry too. Have you been to that new Jamaican spot everyone's been talking about?"

"The one in Wynwood? Nope, but it sounds like the vibe I am looking for."

"Okay great! Come down when you are ready." With a sudden rush of energy, Zolee wound her hips and did a littler shimmy as she danced to the bathroom.

An hour and a half later the two friends were sitting at a small round table while they swayed to the music of the live reggae band and enjoyed their drinks. The alcohol had Zolee feeling good but it only made her miss Cooper more.

"Are you ever going to tell me what happened with you and Ashli's friend or what?" Ari was dying to know what happened after they left her party together. She hadn't even realized they left until the party guests started to thin out. Zolee was usually open with sharing her sex life but it had to be something special for her to want to keep it to herself, which only increased Ari's interest. Zolee pulled her bottom lip between her teeth and blushed. If she was lighter her skin would have flushed red. She stirred her drink with her straw.

"Dang! Can't a girl keep anything to herself?" Zolee rolled her neck and dished out sass.

"Nope, not from her best friend." Ari pouted before stuffing her mouth with jerk chicken. Zolee twisted her lip and looked around before breaking into a huge smile.

"Oh my gosh Ri, Cooper was everything! He made me forget that I was having a one night stand and it felt like I'd known him all my life. That man knew his way around my body. He was seductive, gentle, rough, and dominating all at once. Gosh it was mind blowing. I'm talking multiple orgasms." Zolee looked around then leaned in closer to Ari which caused her to do the same.

"Every time I think about him... my stomach flutters and my pussy throbs. It reacts to him! My pussy reacts to his voice Ari! That's some crazy shit. It's like we exchanged energies. It was some spiritual shit and I need more." Zolee giggled as she played a beat on the table to emphasize her point.

"Aren't you fucking Harry?" Ari narrowed her eyes. Zolee flipped her hair out of her face and scoffed.

"What Harry and I do is far from fucking. We have textbook sex, but I'm done sleeping with him. It's a waste."

"Slow your roll ZoZo. Harry is the first guy you've dated since Lo and let you tell it, he's a good guy. You don't want to mess that up because of a hot and heavy one night stand with Ashli's friend. He's just getting over a breakup from what I hear. You are more than a rebound."

"You're absolutely right. He's um... he's coming for Easter."

"What? Why?"

"What do you mean why? To see me. We agreed to share all major holidays with each other. It was his idea." Zolee gave Ari a triumphant smile and sipped from her glass.

Ari sat back in her seat. She wasn't expecting for them to continue to see each other but then again her friend, when at her best, can have a powerful effect on those she comes in contact with.

"Wow! Okay that changes things. You've obviously had a profound effect on him as well."

Zolee thought about the exciting passionate night that they shared and shook her head. Other than Ari and Ashli she hadn't met anyone that she connected with like she did with Coop. She thought that her and Lo had it but what she had with him wasn't close to how Coop made her feel. Zolee felt hopeful, alive!

"It's like he jump started my heart Ari." She spoke in a hushed tone.

"Yeah I've noticed you've been different. More like your normal self, but even better." Ari smiled as they continued to eat their food. She was excited for Zolee but also worried because Cooper lived in a whole other state. Zolee was tactical and thrived on sight and physical touch but she was glowing, Ari needed to get with Ashli to make sure this didn't end badly.

"I just don't want to get hurt so I am trying to chill."

"All of this doesn't look like your chillin' to me." Ari laughed and waved her hands around me.

"I can't help it! I said that I was trying."

"So he's coming for…"

"Easter."

"Easter? What the hell y'all plan to do? Oooo I know! You can have a yoni egg hunt if you know what I mean. Or do a little bunny hopping!"

"Ari!" Ari and Zolee released a loud laugh which caused all eyes to fall on them. They shushed each other but continued to cackle.

Zolee shook her head and released a long sigh. "You stupid, you know that?"

"Yeah and you love it. Now hurry up we need to do a little shopping to get you ready for Coop!"

Chapter 2

Instead of focusing on the woman he was in bed with, Cooper couldn't get Zolee off of his damn mind and he tried. Even though it was his suggestion that they link up for the holidays she wasn't supposed to occupy his head like she was. Even now while Sasha was bouncing on top of him he could only see Zo. He could only smell Zo; she was in his skin and embedded in his synapses. Fighting not to call out her name Cooper had to bite down on his lip.

"Oh my gosh baby you feel so good. Mmmm yes baby fuck me!" Sasha screamed out and it snapped Cooper temporarily out of the spell Zolee had on him.

"Fuck. That's right bounce on it." Cooper couldn't deny that Sasha was great in bed but he felt so disconnected, like he was a bystander in his own bed. To speed things up Cooper grasped her hips as he pumped into her; it allowed him to hit her spot just right.

"Shit Coop right there. Yes! Yes! Yes!"

Sasha fell on top of Cooper while he laid underneath her, tense. She sighed and started to draw on his chest with her finger. Cooper sat up.

"Get up."

"What? What's the matter? I know you and I know you are all ready for round two." Sasha tried to kiss Cooper but he turned his head which crushed her spirit. He lifted her and slid from under her before he headed to the bathroom. Cooper leaned in the doorway. When he arrived home from his last tour stop Sasha was there waiting for him and like an idiot he let her seduce him. Although he knew that she was no good for him Cooper still loved Sasha and the part of him that hadn't work through his abandonment issues was drawn to the fact that she still wanted him. Sasha wanted him. *Didn't Zolee want him too? There was no guarantee that she was any different.* Cooper sighed and rubbed the top of his head.

"Sasha we can't keep doing this..." Sasha waved Cooper off and chuckled. She sat up on her knees in all her naked glory that Cooper couldn't help but acknowledge.

"We could if you just stay out of your feelings. It was a mistake and I said that I was sorry Coop!"

"Your ass is only sorry because Young Troy dumped your thirsty ass." Cooper kissed his teeth and crossed his arms.

"Really Coop? That's cruel, especially for you. You know what? I'm not doing this with you tonight. I'll be in the guest..."

"Leave." Cooper's voice was eerily calm.

"You don't really want that, do you?"

"LEAVE!" Cooper roared and Sasha jumped from where she now stood then immediately started to put her clothes back on. Cooper locked himself in the bathroom and proceeded to wash any trace of Sasha off of his skin. It wasn't his intentions to talk to her the way he did. He hadn't forgiven her and it was wrong to let her back into his bed; dangerous. Cooper released a deep sigh as the hot water hit his skin. He held his head under the water. The minute his eyes closed Zolee's infectious smile flashed before him. He made a quick task out of showering and slipped on some sweats. Before he could grab his phone and dial up Zolee, Beyoncé's *7/11* began to play from the phone. Cooper licked his lips and smirked as the picture he snapped of Zolee sleeping popped up.

"Would you believe me if I said that I was just thinking about you?" There was a slight pause. Cooper could hear soft music playing in the background.

"Maybe. How are you?"

"Better now that I have you on my line." Zolee let out a soft chuckle then sighed.

"Easter is right around the corner. Did you get your plane ticket?"

"Paid for it today. I switched the days. I fly in that Wednesday night and you have me until the following Tuesday."

"All to myself?"

"You can be as selfish as you want."

"Cool I like that. So tell me Cooper, what do you like to do when you're not working?"

"Other than work out? Uhh, I meet up with my cousin and his boys to play ball, I watch a lot of ESPN, and I volunteer at the rec center."

"So you like kids?"

"Yeah. Don't you?"

"I mean they're alright. I don't really give them a second thought."

Cooper grabbed himself a beer out of the refrigerator and sat on the couch with his legs outstretched.

"Interesting. Zolee doesn't like kids."

"I did not say that Cooper! I'm not around kids that much to say if I like them or not; I'm just indifferent." Zolee's voice squeaked as she spoke. "Damn, my mom's calling me. I should answer that."

"You should. We'll talk later. Goodnight ZoZo."

"Good night Coop. Tomorrow?"

"Always."

"One more time and all out this time guys! FIVE, SIX, SEVEN, EIGHT!"

The music began to play and the dancers began to move in sync to the music. Cooper walked up and down the length of the mirror as the group of dancers executed his choreography for the video that he was hired to choreograph. Thankfully, his career was at the point where people sought *him* out and he was booked for the remainder of the year.

"Come on, pick up the energy! Don't get replaced; you all are professionals and were handpicked for a reason!"

The R&B artist and the star of the video came sashaying in with her small entourage. Queen nodded and smiled as she bopped to the music and studied the dancers. She declined the seat that was offered up and stood against the wall and tried to catch the moves. Cooper would work with her one-on-one to teach her the choreography specifically created for her before having her to rehearse with the dancers. Cooper took in her appearance and nodded his approval. Queen was dressed in high waisted jeans that showed off her curves and hugged her ass nicely. Her crop top barely made it past the underside of her huge, perky breast. Her hair was dyed blue and she wore it in long waves. As Cooper walked over to her he couldn't help but smirk at the way she shamelessly undressed him with her eyes. Her sight landed right between his slightly bowed legs. Cooper nudged her shoulder with his.

"What do you think?"

"I think you are amazing Cooper. I love it! I can already tell that people are going to want to learn the choreography and that is exactly what I wanted."

"Oh no doubt. Dancing in a video is pointless if no one wants to copy the moves." Queen nodded her head has she stared at Cooper. She wanted him and wasn't trying to hide it. He was incredibly attractive; refined, but also a little rough around the edges. and very masculine; she loved that shit.

"When do we start again?"

"Bright and early tomorrow." Cooper smiled at her then focused back on the dancers. "Just make sure you get plenty of rest, eat, and drink plenty of water."

"Wait. Is this bootcamp or practice?"

"Both. I got to get you conditioned. This ain't some basic ass Tik Tok moves Queenie." Cooper winked at her then made his way to the middle of the room to give feedback and close out the rehearsal.

"I usually like to end this on a positive note, but y'all fucking sucked today. Let's regroup and try this shit again tomorrow evening."

On his way home Cooper decided to call up his favorite girl in the world. She picked up almost immediately, her warm cheerful voice put a huge grin on his face.

"Hey son!"

"Hey ma. What's up? How are you and the old man?"

"We are fine, just fine. Your daddy is out at the lake fishing with some of his buddies. I'm praying that he doesn't bring home none of that stinky behind fish for me to cook or I'm going to send him over to you!"

"Nah mom, that's a hard pass." Cooper frowned and scrunched his nose as if he could actually smell fish. He and his mom both hated fish but that didn't seem to stop his dad from bringing it home and cooking it.

"Anyway. He loves to fish so who am I to stop him, you know? As for me I've been in the kitchen all day baking my cakes and pies to sell."

"Mom it's called retirement for a reason."

"Exactly which means I can do whatever the heck I want! Ya mama is still young. I'm not even sixty yet, close, but not there!"

Cooper laughed as he took his exit off the highway. He didn't think anyone would understand how much he loved catching up with his mom. Cooper couldn't remember not ever knowing that he wasn't adopted; his parents had agreed to tell him and educate him about it as early as possible. Not once did they ever make him feel like he wasn't made from their own flesh and blood, even when he was an unruly teen asshole who would sneak out the house, hang with goons, and experiment with drugs. They never gave the impression that they regretted taking him in. Some days he found it hard to believe, but he knew better. Even though he was raised surrounded by love Cooper still lived with the emotional pain of not being wanted by his biological family. He learned to will his emotions away whenever they were too much for him to handle but never came to terms with it.

Lela and Matthew Powers took him in when his mom was only twenty-five years old. His dad was twenty-seven at the time. Eighteen months later he was legally theirs. Lela and Matthew were raised to be hard workers. While his mom worked tirelessly as a nurse, his father worked for the county as a supervisor for the parks department. His mother quit the ER and got a job with a private practice which allowed her to give Cooper the attention he needed. Both of them were now retired and they were living their best life and deserved it.

"I'll give you that. You deserve to do whatever you want."

Cooper could hear utensils and pots clanging, then water running. "Enough of the small talk Coop. How long do we have you this time?"

Coop used his free hand to scratch his head. His work kept him away from home for months at a time. He was Lela and Matthew's only child, so he knew his absence affected them.

"Uhm, another two weeks then I'm back in Miami for a few days, then home for another two weeks to wrap up this video then I'm back on tour until October. After that I'll be back in forth between here and New York."

"You never did want to stay put. Always wanted to be doing something or going somewhere. It's like you've been running your whole life."

Cooper sighed and clenched his jaw. He knew the direction that this conversation was heading and wasn't for it, not today.

"Mom, I- I'm not running. I met a friend in Miami back in February that I'm going to visit *and* I just love what I do. Another perk of my job is that it allows me to travel."

"I know son but you don't spend enough time with your father and I, specifically your father. He would never say anything but being a father to an amazing son is his proudest accomplishment. This may sound cliché but you Cooper are his pride and joy. We miss you baby."

Now he felt guilty. Cooper never wanted his parents to feel like he didn't appreciate them but after finding out that his mother didn't want him he struggled with getting close to other people. There was even a period in his teens when he tried to pull away from them. Most of his relationships were superficial, surface. Ashli somehow wormed her way in, but she was more like family since they grew up together and now there was Zolee.

"I'll do better mom. Matter of fact what are you doing right now?"

"Just put the last pie in the oven and I'm going to make something simple for dinner. Your daddy wanted wings and fries and I'm trying to have dinner ready before he tries to hand me fish to fry."

"Dang ma, you know I love your fried chicken! You couldn't start our conversation with that?" Cooper snickered to himself and used his spare key to let himself into the modest ranch style home. He smiled as soon as he laid his eyes on his mother and she rolled her eyes and ended the call. Cooper hugged her and pecked her on the cheek.

"Hey mom."

"Boy! I told you about playing with me like that." She swatted Cooper with a dish towel before she removed a perfect batch of golden fried chicken from the deep fryer. Cooper salivated and licked his lips. He washed his hands at the sink and finished cutting up the potatoes for his mom. Cooper was not the best cook but he knew how to chop, dice, and prep the hell out of food for cooking. His mother hummed while she worked around the kitchen. Cooper instantly relaxed and fell into his normal rhythm while at home.

"Now who is this friend that you met while in Miami? I assume that it's a new female friend?"

"Damn sure ain't traveling for no nigga. Ouch!" Lela rinsed off the wooden spoon and continued mixing the tea.

"Watch your mouth young man. Now, what happened to that Sasha girl?"

Cooper responded in a dull tone. "Sasha cheated. We're done." Cooper's mom didn't immediately respond as she started frying the potatoes. She finally spoke after a few minutes of silence.

"If it makes you feel any better I always thought that you could do better than her. She had a wandering eye like she was always appraising or looking for the next best thing."

Cooper scoffed with a smug expression on his face. His

thought's immediately when to Zo again.

"You're right about that." His mom regarded him sideways and perked up. Before she could respond the back door opened and his dad stomped in with a cooler. His mom held out her free hand.

"Ut uh! Take that back outside Matthew! Don't bring that stinky ass fish in here until you clean it. You, not me." Cooper's dad leaned forward and his mom met him for a kiss before he backed up out of the door. A minute later he waltzed back in.

"Hey son! Long time no see. Let me wash up and then we can all catch up."

Forty-five minutes later they were in the dining room stuffing their faces with homemade wings and fries. Half of Cooper's wings were plain and the other half were dipped in his dad's famous secret sauce. Cooper had filled his parents in on how the tour was going and his upcoming work projects.

"Tell me about *her*."

"Who mom?" Cooper avoided his mom's eyes and stayed fixated on his plate.

"Miami?"

His dad chuckled and took a swig of his Corona. Matthew new his wife and Lela Powers wanted a daughter-in-law and grandbabies and she wanted it yesterday. She'd been holding her tongue but she was ready to burst.

"Oh. Well her name is Zolee. We met at a party on my birthday and she's actually a friend of Ashli's."

"Is she pretty?" His dad nudged him and laughed.

"She's gorgeous dad. She's attractive both inside and out. Zo is a good girl."

His mom popped a fry in her mouth. "Hmm. I see."

His parents gave each other knowing looks that Cooper didn't miss.

"Come on guys. We barely know each other. We're just having fun." Cooper shrugged his shoulders and stuffed a hand full of fries in his mouth.

"Son you say that you barely know this girl but you're traveling to see her again?" His dad chimed in with a smirk on his face. Matthew took a sip of his beer while he waited for an answer.

"Well how else are we going to get to know each other better?" Cooper sighed in exasperation.

"Aight Coop. When you're ready to talk you know where to find me." Cooper's dad patted him on his shoulder. His dad was never one to drag information out of Cooper. He was patient enough to wait until his son was good and ready. Matthew gave his wife a look that communicated for her to let their son be. She rolled her eyes. His mother stood up to clear off the table and the men got up to help. In the kitchen Cooper loaded the dishwasher while his mom put up the leftovers.

Lately Cooper had been thinking about the woman who gave birth to him. He wondered what she looked like and if he looked like her or his father. More than anything he wanted to know why she abandoned him hours after birthing him. He'd never brought it up before because he didn't want to hurt his parent's feelings, but he was grown now and needed to do what was best for him.

"Umm mom?"

"Yes baby?"

"When I was born was there any information on my mom? Like where she lived or emergency contacts?" Lela's body stiffened but she recovered quickly.

"No baby. From what I remembered she was a young mean little thing and she gave as little information as possible." It didn't go unnoticed that his mother's body tensed at the question; she wouldn't even look at Cooper. Lela started busying herself with wiping down the countertops. She knew who Cooper's biological mother was, but it was her job to protect him. He was *her* son. Cooper tugged her arm to get her attention.

"Mom?"

"What?"

"Okay, what about her full name. Are you sure…?"

"Yes, I am sure Cooper!" Cooper released her and took a step back.

"Sorry, I didn't mean to yell." Cooper regarded her before he released a hard sigh. He looked up to see his father standing in the archway.

"Come on son. Watch the rest of this basketball game with me." Cooper simply nodded and followed his father to the den. He couldn't help the nagging feeling that his mother was holding out on him. She knew more than what she was letting on. Her response only spiked his curiosity, he would get the answers that he was looking for one way or the other.

Spring

Chapter 3

Never did Zolee think she would be out shopping in preparation to cook for another man. She'd only cooked for her ex and her dad, but here she was pushing a shopping cart around the produce section of her favorite grocery store. She scrolled through the list she'd typed earlier on her phone to make sure she had what she needed before she moved on. Since she lived alone there was only enough food to feed one person, so she needed to stock up. Cooper was an active man and she was sure that he ate a lot because, what man didn't eat a lot? Zolee hummed as she picked out items for breakfast, lunch, and dinner, then grabbed snacks, juice, water, beer, and wine. As Zolee turned down the aisle with the coffee and tea, she froze when she smelled a familiar scent.

It can't be.

"Lo! Stop, not in public!" A high pitch female voice shrieked then giggled.

Zolee's heart pounded in her chest and her mouth felt dry. She slowly looked up to see Lo and Kenya standing right in front of her favorite tea. She was holding a box of tea and Lo's face was buried in the crook of her neck. Surprisingly this was her first time seeing him since their wedding day a little over three years ago and her first time seeing Kenya ever, but she knew it was her. Zolee couldn't help but smirk. Kenya was homely looking. She had beautiful long wavy hair, but her face was riddled with acne scars. Zolee knew her mom would be ashamed of her for thinking it but Kenya just wasn't pretty. She was basic. Lo paused as if he could sense Zolee and his head popped up.

"Lee! Wow! Shit! I mean hi. What are you doing here?"

"Same thing everyone else is doing here, well with the exception of you two." Zolee raised an eyebrow and nodded her head in their direction and smiled. Lo looked embarrassed and it made her feel bad for the girl.

"Um err, Kenya this is Zolee."

"Zolee? Oh! Zolee! Um hi." She extended her hand and Zolee didn't even acknowledge her gesture. Kenya could not stop staring at Zolee who's toned legs were on full display in the short denim t-shirt dress she was wearing with a pair of red Converse. Lo couldn't stop staring either.

"You look good Lee."

"Thank you."

"So, how have you been?"

Zolee stared at Lo like he had three heads. After leaving her on their wedding day and never reaching back out, there was no way in hell he really cared about how she was doing. She wanted to kick his face in. Zolee scoffed then barked out.

"Tea!"

"What?"

"Tea. I need my tea and you two are in the way."

Lo turned around and handed Zolee her favorite pineapple hibiscus tea. Kenya glared at him then her. Zolee snatch the box and tossed it in her cart before turning around.

"You don't have to be jealous Lee. I never took you as that type."

Stay calm Zo and keep walking…No this ass didn't! Zolee whipped back around and snarled.

"That's because I am not, especially not jealous of *her* Lorenz. Are you kidding me?" Zolee knew that she was being a bitch but she couldn't help herself. She sized up Kenya and chuckled. "She doesn't even come close to me and you know it. She probably only fucks in missionary."

"Really? Well who's wearing his ring honey?" Kenya smirked while waving her hand at her like she was an extra in Beyoncé's

Single Ladies video.

"Hmph. Oh, that old thing? He couldn't even give you a new ring sweety. Before you wore it, it was on my finger first Ken-ya." Kenya's face dropped but so did Zolee's.

Shit, this girl didn't know. Zolee paused and took deep breaths. *Let it go Zolee Rose Norwood, let it go.* Zolee couldn't let it go. Anger had a hold of her and wouldn't let go until she unleashed. She set her sights on Lo.

"You proposed to her?!" Kenya screamed.

"Proposed and then broke up with me on our wedding day. If you ask me I'd say he's feeling a little nostalgic. He obviously can't keep his eyes off of me. I already know exactly what he's missing and I *definitely* know what you are missing, but he's okay with you faking it I'm sure, just as long as you stroke that ego. Your husband is a grimy ass snake who would cheat on his *best friend* and fiancé then leave her at the alter months after she buried her father! Fuck y'all. Fuck you Lo!" Kenya eye's ballooned and that was Zolee's cue. Her hands were shaking so she kept a firm grip in the cart. She turned around and headed down the aisle.

"Good luck Lo."

"You did not!"

"Yes I did. It was like I was possessed. I knew I was being a petty bitch, but I couldn't stop myself. I all but outright called the girl ugly."

Zolee sipped her wine then refilled Ari's glass.

"When he called me jealous I lost all manners and scruples. I didn't even say half the shit I wanted to say, asshole."

"I would have loved to see her face when you told her you had it first when it came to that ring. That was a nice ring though."

Zolee poked her lip out. "It was, wasn't it?"

Although Zolee almost showed her entire ass in Trader Joe's, she had no significant feelings when it came to seeing Lo with his now wife. He had picked up weight and was dressed just as dowdy as she was. Zolee knew she'd dodged a bullet. There was a knock at Zolee's door and she jumped.

"Dang girl it's your door. Ooo did you call Harry over to get one in before…"

"Bitch what?! Stop Ari."

Zolee looked throughout the peephole and screamed before she made quick work unlocking the door and slung it open. Zolee slammed into Cooper's chest making him almost lose his footing as he caught her and held on. They both laughed. Still holding on to her, Cooper kissed Zolee. He hadn't planned to but it felt right. When she cupped the back of his head and moaned he deepened the kiss until they were interrupted. Ari cleared her throat and Cooper peeped around Zolee in bewilderment. Zolee jumped out of Cooper's arms and stood back, giving Ari a bashful look.

Ari clapped her hands together and grinned. "Oh no, please don't stop on the account of me being here hanging out with my best friend." Ari crossed her arms and smirked at them. She had to admit that they looked cute together. She could see the enthusiasm in both of their eyes. It also made her miss Brandon. He already had her friend wide open and Zo didn't even realize just how much. She was gone. Cooper dawned his crooked smile and nodded in Ari's direction.

"Hey Ari."

"Coop. Good to see you again."

"What are you doing here?! You're a day early."

"I wanted to surprise you. My bad I didn't even consider that you would have been busy. I should—"

"Aww you missed her didn't you?" Cooper and Zolee both stared at Ari expressionless. Ari rolled her eyes.

"Okay I think this is my cue to go home. You two have fun." Ari picked up the unfinished bottle of wine and her other belongings before waving them off and making her exit. Zolee ensured that the door was secured and locked before turning back to Cooper. Her locs were gathered at the top of her head and she was wearing a tank and joggers, her feet bare. Her place smelled earthy, like an Eden, warm, floral, and woodsy. Cooper didn't pay much attention to it the last time he was there but he could instantly tell she was a minimalist. The living and dining area only contained the necessities with only a hand full of decorative items. There were strategically placed plants and art on the wall that looked to be from the same artist.

"You like it?"

"Yeah, it fits you. I didn't pay much attention last time because, well you know." Zolee blushed and pulled the side of her lip between her teeth.

"Shit! Put your um, stuff down I'm sure your tired. Did you fly in from New York?"

"No, I was home in Atlanta so it wasn't a long trip, but I've had a busy few weeks." Zolee reclaimed her spot on the couch and Cooper joined her. Unexpectantly she jumped up from her spot.

"Shit! I'm so rude. Are you thirsty? Hungry? Do you want anything?"

Zolee was nervous, maybe even a little rattled and Cooper found it endearing. Before she could rush past him he stood and pulled her to him. His soft lips pressed into hers before he explored her mouth. She tasted like sangria. Cooper pulled back and Zolee groaned with disappointment.

"Chill. It's just me." Zolee rubbed her hands up and down Cooper's tattooed arms.

"I know. It's just I don't know what to expect."

"How about we don't expect anything. Let's just go with the flow; go with what feels right."

"Coop you know that's hard for me. I like to know what's going on. I don't care for surprises."

"Well you are going to have to let that go when I'm around pretty lady because I'm running the show." Zolee regarded Cooper sideways, she didn't like surprises and always needed the inside info on what was going on.

"What do you have up your sleeve Mr. Powers?"

"Wouldn't you want to know." Cooper released Zolee and chuckled before he grabbed his bag and headed to her room.

"I'm going to take a quick shower."

"You're not going to tell me? Come on! Cooper!" Cooper shot her the peace sign as he swaggered down the hall to her room.

The next morning Cooper quietly watched Zolee as she slept. He studied the rise and fall of her chest, the peaceful look on her face, the way her hair was tousled across her face and the way the sunlight peaked through her blinds and gave her face an angelic glow. It was a whole mood and he committed it to memory. Cooper never felt so at peace, so at home, so in need. Cooper woke up already half-way at attention and Zolee's natural scent only made it worst. With a devious grin he sat up and peppered kisses all over Zolee's face then worked his way down her neck and chest. He pulled her tank up and latched on to her dark chocolate coated nipple; his thick wet tongue swirled around it until it hardened. Zolee arched her back and moaned. He grinned when he felt her hand splay across the back of his head and her manicured nails grazed his head. When she shifted to spread her legs Cooper eagerly crawled in between them.

"Good morning." Cooper reached under his pillow, pulled out the condom, and sheathed himself.

"Cooper, I haven't even brushed my teeth… Mmmm got dammit." Cooper shut her up by slamming into her warm core. She was ready for him. Zolee surrendered to Coop and let him have his way with her. The headboard knocked against the wall as the bed rocked back and forth. Zolee and Cooper's moans filled the bedroom as they sexed each other until their skin glistened with sweat and they were completely drained.

A couple of hours later Zolee was in the kitchen making a late breakfast that consisted of bacon, eggs, and banana nut pancakes. Although she was a little sore Zolee felt good. When she removed the last pancake from the pan. She turned to grab her coffee mug and was startled to see Coop sitting at the counter.

"Shit Coop! Are you trying to scare me to death?"

Cooper tried to contain his laugh but failed as it sputtered out and he bellowed. Zolee narrowed her eyes at him.

"My bad Zo. You were in your zone and I was enjoying watching you work the kitchen."

"Cooking is calming for me. It's another way to create. Did you sleep well?"

"Hell yeah, I haven't slept that good in a long time. Waking up to you was even better."

Zolee sat a plate in front of Cooper and blushed. She leaned over the counter and watched him devour the food.

"I'm sure it was. This is different for me Coop. I've never done anything like this."

"Zo sit down and eat." He never looked up from his plate. Zolee huffed then sat two cups of orange juice and coffee on the counter for her and Cooper before she sat down and joined him. Cooper stuffed a forkful of the pancakes into his mouth and moaned. Zolee giggled.

"Is it good?"

"Hell yeah. Did you make these from scratch?"

"Yep! My mom taught me. It's a family recipe that's been passed down and we all have to put our own little spin on it."

Cooper regarded Zolee with curiosity of something he hadn't noticed until now. Zolee rarely spoke of her mom and they talked about everything.

"You don't mention your mom much. What's up with that?" Zolee shoveled her eggs around her plate and shrugged.

"I don't know. Things have been off with us since she started dating Charles. We used to be close. My dad's death made us even closer, even if I'd become distant specifically around the holidays. We were each other's support. She was the only one who understood my relationship with my dad, so imagine my surprise when she introduced me to the man she'd been dating when I came over for our weekly dinner and girls time. I was devastated. She didn't need to lean on me anymore, she had *him* and I had nobody."

Zolee angrily swiped a tear from her eyes, she hated crying. She stabbed a piece of pancake and shoved it into her mouth.

"What about Ari? You had her."

"Yeah but I couldn't be negative Nancy every time we spoke or linked up. I didn't want to put that energy on her. She's similar to me in that we're empaths. We feed off of other's emotions and that shit can be draining."

"That's how you ended up with the therapist?"

28

Zolee slowly nodded her head. "I'm an introvert, but I love people and I like being around good energy. I love life and everything about it so when I stayed up one night drinking from a bottle of tequila thinking of all the ways that I could kill myself it terrified me. I cried for four days straight until I got up and got help and I can't even tell you how I was able to do it. I actually had to call 9-1-1 and they Baker Acted me."

"Zo. You never told anyone?" Cooper tilted her chin to force her to look at him; his was etched with concern. He felt for Zolee and couldn't imagine her dealing with some shit like that by herself. It was a miracle that she survived that. Zolee took in a shaky breath and gave Cooper a small smile.

"Still haven't, well just you."

Cooper pecked her on the lips then gently tugged at one of her locs.

"Thank you for trusting me."

"Yeah, I find it easy to talk to you. Anyway, enough of this heavy shit. That's what therapy is for. Right?"

"Nah, I'm here too Zo *and* you have a great group of friends who would drop everything to be there for you if you let them. Don't carry that shit alone."

"Alright *Coo-per*. Dang. You're smarter than you look."

Cooper held his stomach as he laughed from deep down in his belly. "Oh really? Tell me how you really feel." Zolee rubbed her hand up and down his arm.

"I'm just playing with you, but I'm not use to having deep conversations with guys. I love that we can talk about anything." Cooper flashed that dimpled smile that knocked down all of Zolee's defenses. She blushed and diverted her eyes back to her plate.

They finished their breakfast and drank their coffee in silence, both deep into their own thoughts. Zolee sighed then pushed back from the counter.

"I hate to do this but I have to get ready for work. I have one shoot lined up then I will be back here to edit and work on some content for social media."

"Its cool go do your thing. I knew you wasn't expecting me until later this evening so I had nothing planned."

Zolee and Cooper worked together to put away any leftovers and clean up the kitchen. Zolee kept sneaking glances at Cooper's bare muscular arms until she got a bright idea and smiled at Cooper.

"Cooper baby?" She leaned into Cooper and purred as she ran her fingers down his solid chest.

"What do you want ZoZo?"

"How do you feel about assisting me today?"

Cooper turned his lip down and shrugged before he smacked her on the ass with the dish towel.

"Let's do it. I don't got shit else to do."

Zolee performed a silly victory dance out of the kitchen and into her room and was still able to turn Cooper on. He grinned and texted his mom to let her know he'd gotten in safe before following Zolee into the room.

Cooper was tired and Zolee was still bouncing around with energy thanks to two large cups of white chocolate mocha. The photo shoot was outside and it was abnormally hot for this time of year, but Zolee handled it like a champ. He was impressed with how seamlessly she ran her business with her team. Everyone knew their role and how she worked so she rarely had to give instructions. Everyone just went into action. Cooper was pretty much the muscle and carried all the heavy shit around. He was cool with it though, he just loved seeing Zolee in her element. She was able to make the amateur model comfortable enough to pull off amazing shots. Zolee knew how to connect with people. She didn't even grasp just how amazing she was.

Back at the condo Cooper decided to give her space to finish up her work and spend some time in the community gym. Also, Sasha kept blowing up his phone so he needed privacy to handle her.

"What do you want?!" He growled into the phone.

"Rude! Is that how you answer your phone?"

"When it's you Sasha yeah. I told you that we were over."

"Oh what, so I'm good enough to fuck when you need your dick wet, but not enough to respect!" Sasha practically screamed into the phone.

"Sasha you lost all of my respect when you fucked another nigga and came running back to me." Sasha was silent. Cooper exhaled has he warmed up on the treadmill. He didn't disrespect women so he knew he was wrong for leading Sasha on. He still had love for her but his heart had hardened towards her.

"You know what Sasha? You're right. It was wrong for me to continue to have sex with you when I had no intentions of repairing our relationship but I can't do this with you anymore. I apologize for leading you on. There's no chance for us."

"Who is she?" She was crying.

"She has nothing to do with what I am telling you. I was good to you Sash and you just shitted all over our relationship and publicly embarrassed me and for what? For that clown ass nigga Young Troy?" He could hear her sniffling through the phone and he cursed himself.

"Cooper even though we were together you were never there. You always had a wall up and would only let me get so close. You are guarded and you passively push people away. This isn't just *my* fault. This has everything to do with your abandonment issues..."

"Don't flipped this on me. You fucked up! Let's count our losses and move on. You take care of yourself, but don't call me or pop up on me anymore."

Cooper didn't wait for a response before he hung up the phone. In the short amount of time that he'd spent with Zolee he realized that he and Sasha would have never lasted. At the time he was blinded by her beauty to see the ugliness in her personality and her ill intentions, but Ashli not liking her should have been enough. He may have been guarded in their relationship but maybe it was because he was never meant to be with her. Zolee was a whole other type of woman; she was a rare breed. He would put her into Jay Cole's category of real women, Nia Long, Lisa Bonet, and Sade. Zolee was fucking mother earth and she had a hold on him that he couldn't shake.

Chapter 4

Dancing with Coop was effortless, he knew how to move his body and command Zolee's to do just about whatever he wanted her to do. They had the crowd's attention and didn't even notice. He and Zolee swayed to the music and moved in time with each other. It was hot out, so their skin shimmered from sweat. They'd spent the morning watching church online and after breakfast they'd dressed and headed for Cooper's surprise.

"Come on Coop what is it?"

"Patience grasshopper You will see."

"What?!" Zolee balled up her face.

"Nothing." Cooper chuckled and shook his head.

Twenty-minutes later they pulled up to the regional park. They passed the huge sign that had The Fifth Annual South Florida Easter Festival printed on it.

"Woooooow," Zolee dragged the word. *"Okay I see you Mr. Powers."*

The festivities were in full swing after they made it to the main pavilion. There was a DJ, a photo booth, food trucks and plenty of arts & crafts. Zolee failed at hiding her excitement and looked up at Cooper with the biggest grin on her face.

After the song ended and the DJ switched it up to cater to the kids, Zolee backed away from Cooper and took in the environment.

"Thank you Coop! I wished I thought to bring my camera."

Taking in everything around them, Zolee pulled out her phone and started taking pictures. She took a few of Cooper and giggled as he posed like he was in a GQ photo shoot. After an hour, Zolee was laid out on a blanket with Cooper sitting next to her. Her face was painted with a rainbow on her left cheek and she was slowly eating cotton candy. Occasionally she'd reach up to feed some to Cooper who for some reason kept looking over his should at one of the many oak trees that shaded the park. An announcement was made over the speaker about an egg drop occurring in five minutes. Cooper tapped Zolee's leg.

"That's our cue."

"For what? What are we doing?"

"What else Zo? We are about to find some eggs." Zolee sat up straight and licked her fingers. Cooper's eyes zoomed in on her mouth as she licked each finger. He licked his lips and wished that it was his mouth instead of hers. Zolee glanced up at him incredulously.

"Seriously? An Easter egg hunt? You really about to have me chasing after eggs with these kids? I'm not trying to fight nobody's mama for pushing a kid and I do fight babies," Zolee said all that with a straight face, which made Cooper laugh. He nudged her with his shoulder.

"Woman bring your crazy ass on."

"I don't even have a basket, this is nuts!"

"I got you. Let's go."

Cooper stood up and pulled Zolee up with him. They jogged closer to the pandemonium that was building up near the middle of the field. A helicopter flew over the open space as the atmosphere buzzed with excitement. Kids jumped in place ready to find one of the few golden eggs hidden, which was typically filled with money. Cooper looked at Zolee and winked.

Zolee muttered, "I can't believe we really doing this shit." But when the helicopter dropped the last round of eggs and the whistle was blown, she took off and blew past Cooper, scooping up candy and plastic eggs while she laughed. After a while Zolee stopped and a joyous look formed on her face. Seeing the delight on all the kids faces warmed her heart. She pulled her phone back out and snapped picture after picture. She moaned at the feel of

Cooper's warm hands as they snaked around her waist and caressed her side. He pulled her into him and whispered in her ear.

"There's a golden egg out there with your name on it and you're warm."

Zolee spun in his direction and her eyes gleamed with excitement. Zolee walked around the field with Cooper guiding her telling her whether she was getting hot or cold. As if a light switch flipped, she turned and found the spot that had Cooper's attention when they were laying out. When she spotted the golden egg her eyes lit up and she jogged towards it. Before Zolee could take four complete steps a blur of a kid shot past her with Coop on his heels.

Shit, he could run! Zolee thought to herself.

Cooper scooped up the rambunctious little boy along with the golden egg. The kid seemed shocked at first but giggled and laughed as Cooper wrestled with him and tossed him around. The little boy who couldn't be more than four years old reached for the egg but Cooper held it from his grasp then squatted so that he was at eye level with the kid. He whispered something to him which made the kid look up at Zolee and make a face as if he was saying *eww*. Cooper pulled a ten-dollar bill out of his wallet and handed it to the little boy before he swiped it from his hand and ran away while yelling, "Thank you mister." Cooper held the egg out to Zolee and grinned from ear to ear. The sun was just starting to set behind him and the blooms from the tree added to make it the perfect back drop. This man was beyond fine; sinfully sexy. Zolee damn near drooled until he said her name for the second time with a chuckle.

"Zolee?"

"Huh?"

"I believe that this is for you." Zolee looked down as Cooper extended his hand out to her. She lifted the golden egg and gently shook it. There was a soft rattle but it gave no hint to what was inside. Cooper licked his lips and nodded his head up towards Zolee. She was dressed in a light blue linen jumpsuit. The thin straps allowed her shoulders and arms to be on full display and like always she seemed to glow in the sunlight. Her locs were wavy from her washing and plaiting it the night before.

Zolee squeezed the bottom half of the egg then lifted the top part that Cooper took from her. She lifted up three sets of beads. There was one that was a pattern of gold beds and amethyst, the other was simply small copper beads, and the third was a combination of translucent brown, orange, yellow, and black beads. Zolee held them up and they twinkled in the sun.

"Are these...?"

"They are waist beads." Zolee had been eyeing them on a local jewelry designer's Etsy account two nights before while the two of them laid around watching BET. She hadn't realized that Cooper was even paying attention to what she was doing; they were the exact ones she wanted. Zolee pulled her lip into her mouth and took a step closer to Cooper.

"Thank you," she whispered before she pushed up on her toes and planted a soft yet sensual kiss on his lips. She didn't care that there were children in bright pastel outfits running around screaming and Cooper obviously didn't either. He leaned into the kiss and parted her mouth open with his tongue. Together they moaned as they got lost in each other. Cooper's hand snaked up her back and to her neck. He gripped her hair and pulled her head back; he knew that turned her on. Cooper kissed her neck then pulled back as he gazed at her with lustful eyes; they were both aroused. He looked down at his pants.

"See what you do to me Zo?" he growled.

"I can fix that," she purred in return.

"Oh I know you will." Cooper scoffed before he tugged her by the arm. They jogged across the field and to the parking lot hand in hand. Cooper opened the passenger door to the Jeep he rented and helped Zolee up and into her seat.

"I am so ready to eat. I am starving."

"Me too." The way Cooper's voice crooned made Zolee whip her head in his direction. Goosebumps tickled her flesh. She raised an eyebrow, her expressions revealing an unspoken question.

"And I ain't talking about food."

"Boy whatever. We've been humping like rabbits since you got here. You ain't have enough yet?" Zolee tried to play off the fact that she was already wet with desire.

"Zolee baby I don't think I can ever have enough of you. Shit, I'll take seconds and all the leftovers."

Zolee tossed her head back and laughed out loud. It was like music to Cooper's ears. He loved that he could put a smile on her face and he would do anything to keep it that way. Cooper told himself that he needed to slow down with Zo but he couldn't stop if he tried.

After a quickie in the shower, Zolee and Cooper were dressed and ready to enjoy her friends and family for the remainder of the evening. Before they left the house that morning for church and festivities at the park, Zolee prepared a red wine marinated pot roast in the slow cooker which she paired up with home-made mashed potatoes and oven roasted broccoli. Ari, along with Zolee's mom and stepdad Charles, joined them and brought along apple pie and ice cream. Zolee's mood had been off since her mother arrived with her boyfriend. She was damn near taking glasses of wine to the head and she practically barked at her mother when she asked to help in the kitchen. Ari was keeping a close eye on her but had yet to act. Cooper couldn't take it anymore after she made another slick disrespectful remark towards her mom. They were gathered in the living area and her mom had lifted up an old family picture.

"I remember when we took this picture. Your father had just brought that car and was so proud. I miss him."

"Shit, could have fooled me," Zolee scoffed and sipped from her wine glass.

"Excuse me?" Zora's delightful expression faded.

"How can you miss him with Mr. Charles sniffing up your ass every time I turn around?"

"Zolee Rose! You of all people know that I will not tolerate..." Her mother's voice shook and she turned her back to Zolee and faced Charles. He massaged her shoulders as he spoke gently into her ear. Zolee rolled her eyes and made a move towards the kitchen.

"Excuse me everyone." Cooper snatched Zolee up by the arm and led her to her bedroom and slammed the door. Zolee snatched her arm away.

"What the hell is wrong with you?"

"Me? What the fuck his wrong with you?" The anger that flashed in Cooper's eyes threw Zolee off and she took a step back, but he was right back in her face.

"All that slick shit you had to say out there to your mom and now you got nothing? What is your problem? You're damn near drunk Zo!"

Zolee's lower lip trembled and she fought to keep the tears at bay. She paced the floor then inhaled and exhaled a cleansing breath.

"I don't want him here! I thought I could do this, but I can't. He... my dad should be here. It's not fair that this man gets to hop right into a ready-made family! A family my father loved, cherished, and worked hard for. How could she think that anyone could replace my dad Coop?" Zolee couldn't hold it in anymore and broke down in loud sobs that surprised even her. She clamped her hand over her mouth in an attempt to hold it in. Her legs felt weak under her and Cooper caught her just in time and held her up. He wrapped his arms around her.

"Before I say my piece let me just say that it's okay. It's okay to feel what you feel because that's real, but you can't ignore that that man out there makes your mom happy. Hell, I can see that shit. Wouldn't your dad want her to be happy? Just like he would want you to be happy?" Cooper's hands now gripped the sides her face as he stared deep into her eyes.

"No, I know Cooper I know this, but it's how it makes me *feel*. I should have avoided the alcohol."

Cooper scoffed and nodded. "You think? You got me and Ari out there. Lean on us, but this is also your mother's first holiday with you since you both lost him. Don't ruin that for her."

Zolee dropped her head and massaged her temples.

"Shit. I was such a bitch. I'm an ass."

"Just in that moment, but you got all night to redeem yourself. Now get your shit together and meet me back out there." Cooper slapped Zolee in the ass then strolled out of the room. After she wiped her face and touched up her makeup, Zolee made her way back to her living area and approached her mom and Charles. She wrapped her mother in a tight embrace and felt her instantly relax. Her mother had also been tensed.

"Guys this isn't easy for me, but I'm glad to spend today with the both of you. Mom I've been a brat and I'm so sorry. That earlier was a about me, not the two of you specifically."

"Yes you were and I accept your apology. Zolee I love you my one and only baby girl. I need you and I will never not need you. We haven't been the same since..." Tears filled up in Zora's eyes but she blinked them away. Zolee loved and admired her mother's strength.

"I know mom and I promise that I am going to do better."

"Tuh! Oh you will because I'm not taking your shit anymore little girl. Next slick comment and I'm knocking those expensive ass teeth clear out, you hear?" Zolee's mouth dropped open and she laughed.

"Mom!" This was the mother that Zolee grew up with. The strong black woman that took no shit from anyone. She had been letting Zolee use her as an emotional punching bag, but Zolee realized it wouldn't have been long before her mother had made good on that threat. Cooper might have just saved her life. As she began to usher everyone to the dining area she mouthed *thank you* to Cooper who winked at her. With the tension finally gone, dinner was filled with the hum of conversations and laughter.

"This was good Zo. I'm glad that my friend is working her way back to normal life because you refusing to celebrate holidays was just depressing." Ari briefly rested her head on Zolee's shoulder before standing up straight. They stood out on the balcony and watched the hustle of the busy city while they sipped their wine. Well Ari was sipping wine while Zolee was drinking coconut water. Cooper was in the house talking with Charles while Zolee's mom cleaned up at her insistence.

"You don't know the half." Zolee looked at her friend before gazing up at the night sky. She wanted so badly to tell Ari everything, all that shit she'd been through with the depression and having to seek professional help, but she didn't want to be treated like she was fragile. Like she would break easily. While her internal life was in shambles, she'd wanted everything else to stay normal, no, she *needed* things to be normal.

"Zo?"

"Huh?"

"I said is there something that you need to tell me? Where did you go just now?"

"It's nothing. I was thinking about where I was a year ago and I never thought that I would feel happy and okay. I feel good RiRi." Ari smiled and twisted up her lips. Zolee was more relaxed and happier. She didn't walk around with that pained expression on her face that she miserably tried to hide. There was a nagging feeling that it was because of that man inside the apartment. Ari watched how Cooper stayed close to her whenever he could and when they were separated, he would watch her, study her. If Zolee was struggling with opening something he would quietly step in; she had been used to doing the heavy lifting on her own for some time now. They interacted like old friends turned lovers. Her friend was feeling Cooper a lot more than she was letting on.

"Does Cooper have anything to do with this?" Ari looked upon her with a sly smile.

"Maybe…" Zolee bumped Ari's shoulder and laughed.

"Come on Zo! Anyone can see it. Spit it out!" Zolee wondered if she talked to her clients that way.

"It's hard to be anything but content when I'm around him. He's just… I don't know. Coop is different, special. Coop is sensitive, doesn't try to hide his emotions, but he is very much alpha male. He don't play that shit and will check me or anyone else if need be. Enough about me though. What about you? How are things with you and Brandon?"

Ari scoffed and took a seat on the patio chair. She closed her eyes for a beat then gazed down at her hand. Zolee didn't like the look on her face so she sat down next to her.

"He's seeing someone Zo." Her voice broke and her bottom lip trembled. "She must be something special because he won't even talk to me anymore. No calls, no texts. I'm blocked from all of his accounts." Zolee would be lying if she said that she wasn't shocked. Ari and Brandon were relationship goals, at least she thought they were. She couldn't believe that he could forget about what they'd been through so easily.

"That's his fucking loss Ari. I'm sorry." Zolee clasped Ari's hand in hers and shook it.

"We were supposed to get married. That was always our plan. I knew we would date other people but this? This wasn't supposed to happen. Can you believe he hasn't told his family? His sister and niece still call me to hang out and I have to find reasons to say no."

"Just because he's being a dick doesn't mean you have to cut his family off Ari. They love you and his niece is basically your niece."

Ari blinked away the tears and smiled at Zolee.

"You're right. Why switch up my life? They are family." Ari always wanted a big family. Her mom was estranged from her own family after getting pregnant with Ari at seventeen, so it has always just been her and her mother. She loved Brandon's family like her own and they even took Zolee into their fold. They loved her.

"Exactly." Zolee clapped her hand on her thigh to emphasize the word then she and Ari clinked their glasses together. They leaned against each other as they took in the energy from the full moon. Zolee released a blissful sigh.

"I'm coming to your class tomorrow night. I need to get my sexy back."

"Oh I got you Ari, trust."

After everyone left, Cooper and Zolee found themselves curled up on the couch watching *Snowfall*. Cooper had been binge watching it and got Zolee hooked on it as well. He was stretched out on the couch and Zolee's small frame was draped on top of him. Her breathing evened out and he knew she'd fallen asleep. He paused the show because he knew she would have a fit if he got ahead of her now that she'd caught up with him. Her phone vibrated on the table next to him. Her phone had gone off several times throughout the time he was there. When she answered, it was either Ashli, Ari, her mom, or work related, but there were times when she checked the screen but ignored the call. Cooper knew it had to be Harry or some other dude. His mind wondered if Harry got to feel what it was like to be buried between her legs and if she dug her nails into his back as she came. The thought had him doing something that was completely out of character. He snatched the phone up and the name on the screen confirmed his suspicions. Cooper swiped to answer.

"My dude she's busy. She'll call you back when I'm done." Cooper didn't wait for a response and ended the call. Cooper knew he was dead ass wrong for doing what he did, but he didn't care. Zolee didn't need to be worried about another nigga on his time. He had two more days with Zolee and he planned to make the most out of it.

Chapter 5

Resisting the urge to call Zolee, Cooper stuffed his phone into his pocket. He was sitting inside of a popular spot in Edgewood having lunch with Ashli. She was talking a mile a minute sharing everything that had happened since they'd last seen each other. Cooper took a big bite out of his turkey burger and stuffed a couple of fries into his mouth.

"We've had an increase in students at the New York location and everyone has been asking about you. Cooper. Cooper are you listening?"

"My bad. I'm listening Ash." Ashli huffed and rolled her eyes.

"Anyways, business is looking good and I received a few emails from artists who wants to work with us on some projects next year." That got Cooper's undivided attention.

"Oh word?"

"Yes! Legends Cooper. If we get this work we will be set for life. They are looking for long term choreographers to work with. I know we're not getting younger but we can make this a deal with the studio. They would have to agree to replace us with one of our employees and we get a percentage. Almost like how modeling firms do for models."

Cooper sat back in his chair and nodded. Ashli beamed as she dug into her salad that she ordered with a side of fries. He didn't understand that shit but to each his own.

"Damn Ash. That's fucking brilliant. Let's get with our people and come up with a solid game plan. Matter of fact…"

Cooper pulled his phone out but was hit with a flying fry.

"Hey! What the hell?"

"We are hanging out today, not working. I only brought it up because I knew that it would get your attention. You got your head up in the clouds." Ashli smirked and looked him straight in the eyes. "Or up ZoZo's coochie."

Cooper tried to hide his smile but lost the battle and his deep dimples made their appearance. Ashli could not help but to smile back. She'd never seen Cooper this smitten with anyone and she was overjoyed that her friend could put that type of smile on his face. She had known for some time that they would be a good match but it was never the right time to introduce them.

"Talk to me, I want details. How are you guys doing? How was your first trip to see her?"

"We are good. We talk or FaceTime every day and the visit was better than I was expecting. Being around Zo is effortless. She's intelligent, driven, and fun to be around. I know she has shit that she's dealing with but she's open and willing to face it head on." Ashli nodded in agreement. Her girl was good peoples and was the holistic, unpredictable, Zen mother of the crew.

"Are you going to be able to let her go?"

"What?" Cooper stopped eating and frowned.

"This agreement that you two have was just for a year, right? What happens after the new year?"

"I don't know." Cooper hadn't considered what would happen after they celebrate their final holiday. He felt like someone had popped his balloon. His eyes roamed around the restaurant as he considered life without Zo's friendship. He couldn't even remember what it was like without it. Cooper sniffed then took a sip of his drink.

"A friendship has been built at this point; we have a bond. It just doesn't end because we accomplished what we said we would do."

A group of women walked by their table and all eyes went to Cooper. He grinned and nodded his head up at them. Ashli rolled her eyes and tilted her head to the side as she stared down the women.

"Excuse me? Don't you see he's with company? Damn!"

"Stop trippin' sis."

"What if Zolee thinks that it should end?" Ashli questioned, regaining Cooper's attention. He shrugged and furrowed his brows.

"Then I would just have to convince her otherwise."

"And what exactly are you convincing her of? Do you want more than a friendship? You have to know exactly what you want Coop. Zo is also my friend and I won't let you string her along just because you want her to yourself. You need to be sure and honest about what type of relationship you want with her."

Cooper rubbed his hands down his face and regarded his best friend. He knew he wanted Zo, but he wasn't sure if he was ready to be on some long-term forever shit right now and that was the type of woman she was. Zolee was the girl you took home to your parents and wife'd up. Cooper also didn't know if he deserved someone as special as Zolee. He wasn't saying that he was incapable of love but could he love her the way that she deserved? Did he have it in him?

"Don't give yourself a headache thinking too hard sir." Cooper's middle finger punched the air and they both laughed out loud.

"Man fuck you Ash."

"I'm just saying." Ashli wiped her mouth then clapped her hands twice. "Time to put in some work at the studio. Let's go with your caramel The Game looking ass."

Cooper tossed money on the table then guided Ashli towards the exit.

"Your ass got jokes now, I see."

"I got an MCM bag full of them. Teaches you not to go so long without seeing your best friend."

Cooper held up the wall while Ashli took over the rehearsal for tonight. They were currently working with the dancers. Ash had switched some things up to help the current routine they were practicing flow better. They both had two different styles of dancing but it always worked perfectly when they created together. Cooper committed each move to memory and nodded his head to the music. Queen's rehearsal didn't start until seven but she'd arrived early and appeared to be pouting. She kept glancing up at Cooper while her assistant spoke to her holding an iPad. Cooper's phone buzzed and he took his attention off the dancers to see who it was. It was a picture of Zolee wearing black skintight leather pants and a dark purple crop top. Her waist beads look good against her skin.

Zo Baby: Guess who Ari didn't have to beg to go out tonight?

Cooper: Word? You looking like you're about to hurt some feelings tonight.

Zo Baby: Oh I intended to…

Cooper: So, what's the play?

Zo Baby: Pregaming then walking over to Brick for dancing and more drinks. What are you doing?

Cooper: Rehearsal. Y'all be safe.

Zo Baby: Always. I'll let you go. Talk later?

Cooper: Definitely. Tomorrow?

Zo Baby: Always!

"Who has got you grinning like that? I'm jealous."

Cooper's head shot up and he was face to face with Queen. She smiled then bit her bottom lip. She looked him up and down without a care in the world. Queen was beautiful but she looked just like any other woman in the industry; cookie cutter. The only thing that set her apart was the blue hair. Cooper was attracted to individuality.

"You're early." His voice sent erotic chills down Queen's spine. She imagined Cooper's smooth voice whispering all types of nasty shit in her ear and all the things she could do with him. It didn't go unnoticed that he had ignored her probing. She wanted Cooper and was curious if he was seeing anybody.

"I am early but you didn't answer my question. I guess it was nobody."

"Nah she's definitely somebody."

"Oh. I didn't mean—"

"Nah you're good. Let me and Ashli wrap this up so we can get started on you." Cooper brushed past Queen and proceeded to close out rehearsal.

"You be careful with that one Cooper." Ashli slipped on her jacket and grabbed her bag.

"What? Who? Queen?"

"Don't play dumb with me. I see how she looks at you and you have a history of falling for her type. You let them worm their way into your heart."

"That's not going to happen Ash. Don't you have a date to be getting ready for?"

"Yeah but I can cancel and stay here with you. Queen is practically ready to drop to her knees and swallow—"

"Hey, chill tiger!" Cooper laughed and guided Ashli towards the door. "Trust me I know how to handle women like her. Call me when you leave and when you make it back home."

"Hey wait. How's the search for your biological mother going?"

"Absolutely nowhere. I can't get a lead on her or anyone she's connected to."

"Did you ask your parents?"

"I asked my mom and I hate to even say this out loud but I think she's lying to me. I didn't like the way she avoided my eyes when she said that she had no idea who my real mother was. She's hiding something Ash."

"Maybe it's best that you don't know." Ashli had a gut feeling that Cooper finding his mom would hurt him more than it would help him. She secretly hoped he wouldn't find her. In her opinion he lived a great life. Matthew and Lela provided Cooper with a loving home and he didn't need to seek this woman out. Cooper released a rush of air and shrugged.

"I have to see this through. I'm tired of wondering. I think about it all the time. I even dream about this shit Ash. You don't know what it feels like to see people and wonder if they're any kin to you. It's haunting me. I need to know so I can move on. We can talk about this tomorrow after you tell me about this nigga you letting take you out tonight. Get out of here."

"Okay. You be safe and be careful." Ashli issued Cooper a silent warning with her eyes then hugged him before she exited the studio. Cooper entered the main room and clapped his hands to get Queen's attention. She turned around and flashed a flirtatious smile. She was dressed in a black leotard and matching fishnet shorts. There was no room left for the imagination. This girl was trouble.

"Alright Queenie. Let's get started."

Summer

Chapter 6

E motions always ran high for Zolee this time of the year. It was her father's birthday and it would be the first one that she didn't spend drunk, high, depressed, or alone, but she was still grieving and she still wanted a drink. This year she made plans to visit his grave site with her mother and she was glad that Charles who she now referred to as Charlie didn't offer to escort them. Although she'd warmed up to him and they were forming their own bond, Zolee needed this time with her mom; they needed it.

Before heading to the cemetery, they decided to eat at her dad's favorite restaurant. Zolee surprised her mom by reserving their normal booth. Zolee sat on her side and her mom sat opposite of her and slid all the way over to leave room for where her husband would have sat. They'd gotten their drinks and were waiting on their entrees. Zolee sat quietly and stirred her Arnold Palmer. Zora kept taking glances at Zolee. She kept fidgeting in her seat and look like she was battling something internally. She knew Zolee. Afraid that her daughter would mentally slip away from her again, Zora was the first to speak.

"I miss that man so much Zo. There's not a second that goes by that I don't think about him, smell him, or feel his presence. I feel so blessed that I got to experience that type of love and happiness. He was a good man, a good father. He was *my* best friend. Was it always easy? No but I never questioned your father's love and he adored his one and only baby girl."

Zora reached across the table and clasped Zolee's hand to get her attention. She had been looking into her glass the entire time watching the ice swirl around. With a deep breath she looked at her mother with tears pooling in her eyes. She angrily swiped away the tears.

"Mommy it's just not fair. I miss him so much. Losing him changed me."

"I know baby."

"No you don't."

Zolee forcefully shook her head. Her hand shook and her mom held on tighter. Her mom deserved to hear her truth no matter how hard it was for her to open up about it. Zolee and her therapist had talked about how she would never fully heal if she continued to avoid this conversation with her mom. "Mom I... I um suffered from depression. It was so bad that I didn't sleep or eat. I just drank because I felt so alone without daddy. There was a point where I considered just ending it all, but I got help." Zolee piped up and squeezed her mother's hand. Tears trickled down Zora's face and she sniffled; she was in disbelief.

"I'm seeing a therapist and I'm doing better now."

Tears continued to flow down Zora's face and broke Zolee's heart. "Baby I'm so sorry you had to go through that alone. You should have never went through that by yourself Zo. I'm your mother. I- I should have known. I should have sensed something. When? Why...?"

"It was right after I found out about you and Charlie. I didn't know how to grieve with someone who seemed so content. I didn't want to burden you because no matter how upset I was I wanted you to be happy. That's why I pulled away from you. This was a secret that I'd been keeping from almost everyone. The only other person who knew was Coop. I need you to understand that I didn't share this to make you feel ashamed or guilty. It's part of me healing and repairing our relationship."

Zora leaned over the table and Zolee met her halfway to receive a kiss on the forehead. "Thank you for trusting me enough to share. So Cooper knew, huh? He must be something special. I see the way you look at him." Her mother smirked.

"Yeah he's special. That man has such a comforting spirit. I was sharing my secrets with him before I could stop myself. He makes me feel hopeful of what's to come."

"Does he treat you well?"

"Yeah, but we're just friends."

"So you and Cooper are *not* having sex?"

Zolee choked and her drink sputtered out of her mouth. She grabbed a napkin and wiped her face and hands. "Mom!"

"Don't play me little girl. You may be grown but I'm your mother and I still know you. I also know how two people look and act around each other who've been intimate. I'm not judging Zolee. Just making an observation after you fed me that *just friends* crap." Zolee was not trying to have this conversation with her mom. She took time to clean the table of the liquid as she tried to stall. She perked up when she saw the waitress making her way over.

"Oh look! Our food is here!"

Zora chuckled at her daughter. She had to admit that Zolee was almost back to being the person she was before her heart was wrecked with loss. The server laid out plates of ox tails, fried chicken, macaroni and cheese, yams, and collard greens. It was a tradition to share their food, so the mother and daughter was sure to order something different. While enjoying their meal the mother and daughter duo laughed, shared memories, caught up with each other, and healed.

Samson T. Norwood
Loving Father and Husband
Forever in Our Hearts

Zolee's hand aimlessly rubbed over the grave marker as she read the inscription over and over again. Her head hung low and the tears wouldn't stop falling. She and her mom decided to give each other individual time, so Zora waited for Zolee underneath the gazebo.

"Daddy I miss you so much. Things haven't been the same since you left. You broke my heart. I went through a little rough patch, but I'm better now. I'm back to working and hanging out with Ari and Ashli, when she's visiting. I know that you're happy to know that all of my *crazy* jobs allow me to live comfortably without having to ask mom for help. You would love the work I've been producing. Oh! I met a guy." Zolee bit her bottom lip and smiled.

"Cooper. Cooper reminds me of you in how he cares for people. I think that's what drew me to him. He makes me feel secure. He's so good to me daddy and I just wished that you could have met him."

Zolee's bottom lip trembled and heart constricted. She gasped and clutched her chest. She felt herself about to hyperventilate but was able to control it by taking long deep breaths. She buried her face in her hands. "God I just want him back. Please, please bring my daddy back!" Zolee broke down and her body shook with sobs. "Daddy I need you."

She could hear what sounded like someone jogging in the grass. His scent greeted her before he did. Cooper sat down next to her and pulled her in his lap. His hand moved up and down her back.

"Coop?"

"Shh. It's okay. Let it all out. Don't leave here holding on to what you've been carrying. I'm here." Zolee wrapped her arms around Cooper and held on tight. Her tears soaked the shoulder of his shirt. She absorbed all the strength and good vibes that he was giving her until the tears subsided. She pulled away and wiped her eyes, a small smile creeped up on her face.

"What are you doing here?"

"Now you know that we wouldn't let you do this by yourself."

"We?" Zolee looked at Cooper with confusion etched on her face. Cooper grinned and pointed towards the gazebo. Ari and Ashli were sitting with her mom talking. They waved when they noticed them looking.

"Are you ready?"

"Yes." Zolee shook her head and smiled. "Just give me a second." Zolee bent over the grave marker and kissed her father's name and she whispered, "That's him dad."

"Thank you guys for being there for me!" Zolee had to shout a little to talk over the music. After getting her mother home and going to Zolee's to freshen up, the crew took Zolee out to happy hour. She was on her second blue long island and already a little tipsy.

"Where else would we be? As long as you have us you'll never go through the hard shit alone." Ari placed an arm around Zolee and kissed her on the cheek. Ashli toasted with Zolee and nodded. Cooper sat across from Zo. He was still worried about her and her decision to drink today of all days, so he made it his job to keep a close eye on her tonight.

"Just like when we fucked up Lo's BMW." Ashli blurted out and Ari gave her the death stare. Ashli slapped her hand over her face and Zolee's mouth dropped open.

"Ah hell, my bad."

Zolee slapped her hands on the table. Cooper just looked on and shook his head. "Wait! You did what? How did I not know about this?"

Ari stirred her drink with the straw and shrugged. "We didn't want to incriminate you in the event that Lo's bitch ass was a snitch."

"It would be a lie for me to say that I can't believe y'all, but you two have always been my ride or die bitches." The three laughed at some inside joke that had Cooper looking confused.

"Do I want to know?"

"Noooo!" The all replied in unison.

The DJ slowed things down and started spinning some old school nineties R&B. The lights dimmed and the vibe shifted. People on the dance floor magnetically became pairs and grooved to the music. Zolee's eyes connected with Cooper's and they both smiled. Memories from February 14th replayed in their minds. A deep voice rumbled over Zolee and she jerked back.

"Hey beautiful." He attempted to grab her hand and lead her on the dance floor without even asking. Cooper pushed the stranger's hand away from Zolee before he could touch her. *He dared him to touch her.*

"Nah."

"Man ain't no one talking to you. Let the lady answer. So you gon dance with a real one or stay posted up here with this nigga?"

Cooper's nostrils flared and he clenched his fist before he slowly stood up. Ashli jumped up and tried to get his attention.

"Hey! Not here Coop." Cooper wanted nothing more than to smash the guy's face in. He felt protective over the girls, especially Zolee, it was almost primal. He released a low growl and the dude frowned. Cooper then shook his head and released a low menacing laugh which put Ashli on alert. She started grabbing their things because she knew Cooper was about to tear shit up. Before Cooper could make a move he was assaulted with the smell of Flower Bomb perfume and gentle arms that wrapped around his waist.

"I choose you." Cooper's heart constricted upon hearing those words; his stomach fluttered and his body was consumed with warmth. He blinked then looked down at Zolee as she leaned into him until he backed up. Zolee then grabbed his hand and led him on the dance floor. He glanced back at the table to make sure that Ari and Ashli were okay before he got lost in the chocolate goddess who somehow was able to quickly calm him down with just a touch and with one phrase that she had no idea of the profound impact it had on him. They tuned everyone out and swayed to the music. They communicated without words and Zolee continued transferring positive energy into him; healing Coop with her touch. The two of them remained that way until the DJ switched it up with a little soca and afrobeat. Ari and Ashli joined them on the dance floor. By then the incident was in the back of Cooper's mind and they all laughed and danced until the lights came on. Spending time with her friends was exactly what Zolee needed. She was appreciative that they'd never given up on her. As long as she had them and her mother, nothing else mattered.

Chapter 7

Dancing in her seat while she waited for the rows ahead of her to exit, Zolee couldn't hide her excitement. The person in the seat next to her glanced at her and smiled. Everything appeared to be happening so fast. The year was less than halfway done and things were still going smooth with her and Coop; it was almost effortless. She kept waiting for the other shoe to drop and for Cooper to reveal his true self that would end up disappointing her but he'd remain consistent. Zolee was teeming with enthusiasm. This would be her first time visiting with Cooper and she was glad to get away from home. She had been working off of fumes and needed the time off, no matter how short it was. When Zolee got off the plane she quickly followed the exit signs as she pulled her carryon behind her. The Atlanta airport was so huge that she had to take a train to the other concourse.

"This is ridiculous." She mumbled when she exited the train and took the escalator down. Zolee checked her phone to see if she'd gotten a response from Coop. She'd texted him from the plane to let him know that she'd landed safely but he hadn't responded. He wanted to pick her up from the airport but she declined and told him that she would call a car service. Zolee didn't see a reason for him to be unnecessarily tortured by the Atlanta traffic. Zolee maneuvered around people with her focus on where to go for pick up. She checked her phone one more time and when she looked up she released a sigh and smiled. Cooper was standing near the doors holding a sign with her name on it. He looked handsome wearing dark blue cargo shorts that hit just passed his knees with a grey t-shirt that hugged his muscular chest and arms. He donned a pair of camo print Vans on his feet. Cooper could make casual look so effortlessly sexy. Zolee picked up her pace and found herself running to his open arms. She slammed into Cooper which caused him to take a couple of steps back to catch his balance. They hadn't seen each other since he'd visited for her father's birthday and they were so busy the last month that they only video chatted once and resorted to keeping up via text. He was touring and she was getting more photography gigs. Cooper spun Zolee around and planted a wet kiss on her lips and made her yoni do the one-two step.

"Damn baby. What's up?" Cooper rubbed his hands up and down Zolee's arms. She was wearing a gray jogger set with silver Converse. Her locs were pulled up in two buns and her face was free from makeup. Zolee smiled then hugged him tightly and they both sighed, not realizing how much they'd missed being in each other's presence.

"How was your flight?"

"It was fine. What's better than stale air and germs?" Zolee shrugged. "I'd missed you Coopster."

"I missed you too and don't get use to calling me that shit!"

"Why? I think it's cute," Zolee whined. Cooper gave Zolee a dead pan look then glanced around her. He frowned at her colorful printed suitcase.

"Is that all you brought?"

"Yep, believe me I have everything I need packed in this baby."

When they made it to the car, Cooper lifted her suitcase to put it in the trunk of his black on black Range Rover. He realized she definitely packed everything she needed. That little suitcase was heavier than it looked. Zolee was already settled in, her jacket tossed across the back seat, so when he closed the trunk, he slipped in on the driver's side.

"You wasn't playing when you said you packed everything that you needed. What the hell is in that thing?"

Zolee examined her royal blue nails. "I've learned how to fit a lot in my carry on. Got that shit down to a science."

Zolee relaxed in her seat as Cooper maneuvered his way out of the airport and onto the interstate. She looked out the window checking out the scenery, which was pretty much a bunch of trees, but there was something peaceful about it. Cooper spoke and captured her attention again.

"I was thinking that instead of staying in Atlanta we could hang out at Lake Lanier. I have a vacation property there."

Zolee was impressed and couldn't help but nod her approval. "Vacation property? Okay big money. How much property do you own Cooper?"

"Just three."

"Dancing has really been good to you, huh?" Usually Cooper would get defensive when a woman brought up the topic of money, specifically his money but Zolee's question was out of genuine curiosity and not ulterior motives. She wasn't adding up numbers in her head. Cooper knew that look all too well. It was the same look Sasha had when they first met and he ignored it like an idiot.

"More like choreography has been really good to me."

Zolee nodded. "So you actually stay on the lake?" Her eyes sparked with excitement. She was used to beaches and hadn't been to an actual lake, let alone a lake house.

"Yes Zo." Zolee bounced in her seat and Cooper couldn't help but smile and move to the music. Her excitement was contagious. By the time they pulled up to the craftsman style house it was close to sunset and Zolee was knocked out. Cooper gently shook her.

"Zo! Zo, wake up!" Zolee stirred in her seat and her eyes fluttered open.

"Huh? Are we there yet?"

"Yes. Now come on! I don't want you to miss the sunset. Grab your camera."

Zolee jumped out of the car, grabbed her purse, and her camera bag. She took in the off white house trimmed in gray with an oak door, as she quickly followed Cooper in the house and giggled at the site of him pulling along her suitcase. Stepping into the house Zolee stopped in her tracks and her mouth fell open. The color scheme carried over into the house with the gray walls, hardwood floors, and black accents. It looked professionally decorated but still felt warm and inviting.

"Are you kidding me? This looks like Chip and Joanna Gaines worked on this house. Did you design this yourself?"

"I gave some input but I hired someone."

"If I lived somewhere like this I would never leave." Zolee spoke as she walked towards the opposite end of the house. Almost the entire wall was windows and had a perfect view of the lake. Cooper followed her as if they were bound together by some invisible chain. When she moved, he moved. While she stared out of the window he unlocked the door and signaled for her to follow. Zolee immediately started taking picture after picture and even snuck a few of Cooper. She pulled out her cell phone and took a selfie of them with the sunset as their backdrop.

"Damn you really are good at this." Cooper swiped through the pictures. They lounged on the patio furniture as they watched the sun set, painting the sky with colors of blue, pink, yellow, and orange. It looked like something from a painting. The sound of crickets trilled around them and, mixed with the cicadas and frogs, created mother nature's symphony. The sun came closer to fully setting. Zolee's eyes glazed over was she watched the colors evolve. When she drew in a shaky breath Cooper put his arm around her and pulled her closer. They stayed like that until the night sky glimmered with twinkling stars.

"My dad and I use to drive out west to see the sunset. I felt his presence today." She turned around to face Cooper. Is that crazy?"

Cooper kissed the top of her head then rested his chin on top. "No. It only makes sense that you would feel something like that. That's the best thing about memories; you can always turn back to them when you feel there is a void."

Zolee slowly nodded her head before she turned to face Cooper again.

"So what's for dinner? Are you cooking?"

"Nah, I can't cook."

"Cooper! I was supposed to cook this time as well?"

Cooper smirked and rubbed her thigh. "Only if you want to, but I was just planning to order out. The kitchen is stocked with water, juice, liquor, bread, and eggs." Zoe stood up and headed into the house towards the kitchen.

"Just like a dude," Zolee mumbled. She opened the fridge then cut her eyes at Coop.

"Fine, I will make a run to the store."

"I can go with you."

"I can manage you just relax, get comfortable and familiarize yourself with the place."

Cooper grabbed his keys and wallet, then kissed Zolee on the lips. She quickly wrapped her arms around his neck and held him in place. She pushed her pelvis against him and the feel her warmth made him brick up. With a lustful smile on his face he wiped remnants of her lip gloss from his mouth and stepped back.

"Keep messing around Zo and I will say fuck food, then have that ass bent over that counter."

Cooper slapped Zolee on the ass before he quickly made his exit. Zolee grabbed a warm bottle of water from the pantry and downed half of it. This was only her second drink of water for the day. Usually by this time of day she'd drank at least sixty ounces of water. She quickly finished the one in her hand then grabbed another bottle that she would just sip on to stay hydrated. Zolee kicked off her shoes then padded around the one-story home. She was impressed. As she toured the home she came across a room that looked like a dance studio. There was a wall covered with mirrors and the floors were hardwood like the remainder of the house. On the walls were pictures from various tours Cooper had been on. The shots captured his physical strength, sexiness, and undeniable passion for dancing. Zolee came across a hallway bathroom and a guest room with its own bathroom before she made it to the master bedroom. In the middle of the room was a king-sized bed with tan and navy blue linens. The wall the bed was against had hard wood planks going across. The room was dark but felt calm. It smelled like Cooper. Before Zolee could check out his closet and the bathroom there was a knock at the door. Confused on who it could be she jogged down the hall to the front door. Through the peephole she could see that it was a woman. Zolee frowned and pulled the door open. The woman was tall and slim but based on her body Zolee easily recognized a fellow dancer. She wore her honey blonde hair in a short blunt asymmetrical bob. She was a lighter tone than Zolee and was dressed in a red maxi dress with gold high heeled sandals. The mysterious woman turned her nose up at the site of Zolee. All of a sudden Zolee felt frumpy in her airport attire. *What the hell Zo? This ain't like you!*

Zolee cleared her throat and spoke.

"Yes? Can I help you?" The uninvited guest looked Zolee up and down before she rolled her eyes.

"Is Cooper here?"

"Um no and you…"

"Oh! Are you renting the lake house for the holiday? He and I usually spend Independence Day here together in that nice big bed of his."

Sasha knew that she wasn't a renter. She'd seen pictures of them together on Facebook and Instagram. She knew she was a friend of Ashli, who was always a bitch to her. Zolee gazed upon the nameless woman with amusement then grinned.

"No. I'm *here* with Cooper. *We* are spending the holiday together. He made a run to the store to get food."

"*You're* here with Cooper?" Sasha looked at Zolee like she was a wad of gum stuck to the bottom of her shoe.

"Yes and you are?"

"Sasha." She huffed and brushed her hair out of her eye.

So, this was Sasha. The silly clout chasing ex-girlfriend that cheated on him with a celebrity that didn't want her, Zolee thought to herself. She was pretty but she and Zolee were night and day so, it made her wonder what Cooper's real type was.

"Well are you going to let me in?"

Zolee crossed her arms and leaned on the door frame. She

looked at Sasha like she was crazy. "No." Sasha's mouth fell open and she placed her hand on her hip.

"No?"

"No, Cooper is not here and I don't know you. Besides, *this* holiday was promised to me. I'm sorry but you will have to find other plans. I'll tell Cooper you stopped by. Before Sasha could reply with a rebuttal, Zolee slammed the door in her face. Zolee didn't like Sasha. She didn't like the idea that someone wanted to take what was hers away from her. *But Cooper wasn't hers. Was he?* Zolee stalked to the kitchen and flung cabinets open until she found what she was looking for. She poured a shot of whiskey and tossed it back. After a second shot, she decided to take a shower and put on something more comfortable to relax her irritated nerves. Zolee snatched up her bag and stomped off to the bathroom where she showered then gave herself a quick facial. It did nothing to improve her mood. She let Sasha push her buttons. It made her feel territorial over Coop. She never wanted to come face to face with someone who was just as or even more familiar with Cooper than she was. It was unnerving. Nearly washing her skin raw Zolee finally snapped out of her trance when she heard the alarm beep to signal that the front door had been opened. She made a quick task of putting on lotion and getting dressed. She slipped into some soft cotton shorts and a t-shirt. The scent of hot cheesy pizza teased Zolee as she made her way to the kitchen. Cooper gave her that smile that always made her yoni pulse, but she didn't smile back. Cooper continued putting away food and gave her a quick glance.

"You alright?"

"Yep."

"I brought pizza."

"I see." Cooper glared at her suspiciously.

"It's your favorite."

"I know."

Cooper let the cabinet slam. "Zo."

"What?" Zolee snapped as she tapped on her phone. Cooper tapped the counter to get her attention.

"Talk to me because I know your ass don't like eating when you're mad, so what happened in the last hour that has you—"

"Sasha was here."

Cooper's body tensed up but his face was expressionless. Zolee scoffed at his perfect poker face. Cooper was a ladies man and he obviously knew how to handle himself in these precarious situations. She could see the wheels turning in his head.

"What did she say?"

"Really Coop?" Zolee turned to walk away but Cooper came around the counter and grabbed her.

"Stop Zo. I'm not with that girl so what did she say she wanted?"

"You! She was coming to spend the fourth with you because that's what you two do every year." Zolee mimicked Sasha which Cooper found pretty impressive. "Are you still fucking her?"

"What?" Cooper reared his head back like he'd been slapped.

"ARE YOU FUCKING HER COOP!" The thought of Cooper with anyone but her was making her come unhinged. These emotions were new for her; she'd never been the jealous type.

"Zo, you know what? You are un-fucking-believable."

"How you figure?"

"Are you fucking Harry?" Zolee opened her mouth to respond and immediately closed it.

"Exactly." Cooper took a step back. He wanted to break something. He fought not to visualize another dude pleasuring Zo. Cooper counted down until he could think straight again.

"Not since before Easter. Now please answer my question." Zolee gritted between her teeth. Cooper glanced at her in disbelief but when he saw the uncertainty in her eyes, it softened him up. He sighed.

"Not since before Easter, then I cut it off," Zolee winced. That meant that he slept with her after Valentine's day and before their first visit. Zolee massaged her hands.

"Do you want to be with her?"

"No Zo, I don't." Cooper shook his head and took a step closer to her.

"Have you slept with anyone else since Easter?"

"No. You?"

"No." Cooper nodded. He felt a sense of relief. Zolee wrung her hands then rubbed them down her thigh. "What are we doing Coop?"

"I don't know. It's not supposed to get complicated."

"You think *this* is making things complicated?"

"No. Yeah…. Shit I think it creates the perfect environment for it. We're supposed to be having fun, not worried about who the other spends their time with."

Zolee pulled at one of her locks and swayed from side to side. She was mumbling something to herself that Cooper couldn't understand so he just put away the rest of the groceries and placed the pizza in the oven to keep it warm. As he grabbed a Corona out of the refrigerator Zolee spoke.

"What if I don't want you to spend time with anyone else?" Cooper paused with the bottle in midair. As affectionate as Zolee was she never gave any hints that she wanted more so he questioned if this was more about her seeing Sasha and not so much her wanting to be with him.

"I think you need to get out of your feelings about Sasha and take a step back." Zolee shook her head and approached Cooper. She wrapped her arms around his waist and tugged until he stepped closer. She stretched on her toes and kissed Cooper. It was soft and cautious at first then she slipped her tongue between his and fervently explored his mouth. Cooper caught himself right before he moaned. Zolee could make him feel so out of control at times.

"What if I don't want you to spend time with anyone else?" Zolee stepped back then stripped down until she stood naked with her breast heaving up and down. Cooper released a growl before he scooped her up and carried her to the couch. He made her get on her knees with her back facing him. After he shed his last item of clothing he gripped her neck and bent her over. Zolee gripped the back of the couch just as Cooper slammed into her. They both released a collective sigh and Cooper wasted no time pulling back out then slamming into her. Cooper used her body to work through his aggression. He never wanted to do that with her but he needed the release. Zolee screamed then whimpered. They spent the next hour using each other's body to work through their frustrations, insecurities, and their insatiable need for each other. Afterwards they'd made their way back to the kitchen to finally eat dinner; Cooper in boxer briefs and Zolee in her bra and panties.

"Zolee, about what you said earlier..." Cooper stopped when Zolee held up her hands.

"How about we just put that on hold so the both of us can process whatever that was?" Zolee raised an eyebrow and reached for a second slice of the spinach alfredo pizza. Cooper nodded and took a sip from his water.

"Alright, cool." He proceeded to stuff half of the pizza into his mouth. Zolee looked on with her eyes wide and her mouth open. It amazed her how much food he could quickly put down. This man barely had an ounce of fat on his body but put food down like a garbage disposal. He would even eat any leftover food off of her plate whenever she wasn't extremely hungry.

"It's not fair that you can eat that much and maintain that physique."

"That's only because I work my ass off every morning and sometimes evenings at the gym. You're more than willing to go on a jog with me in the morning."

"I might have to; with the way you already have me eating."

"Yeah but I got plans to help you work that off."

Zolee blushed when Cooper kissed her on the cheek. He picked up their paper plates and tossed them in the garbage. She'd realized that she was acting crazy earlier after Sasha made her appearance, but Cooper didn't let it bother him for long. Zolee felt her eyes grow heavy. She'd had a long day and was tired. She blinked a few times to keep her eyes open. Cooper moved around the kitchen with ease as he cleaned up their mess. He reminded Zolee a lot of her dad. Her dad was the kind of husband that helped with the cooking, cleaning, and household work. He wasn't the type of man to consider it *women's* work; if he could help then that's what he did. Her parents were a team.

"Tell me more about your parents."

Cooper smiled and led Zolee to the room. He'd noticed her yawning and fighting to stay awake. He was also still trying to figure out what Sasha said or did to get Zo so riled up. Her reaction earlier was out of character, but Sasha knew how to push buttons. Cooper sat in the chair in the corner of the room near the large window and rested his feet on the ottoman.

"Lela and Matthew Powers are two of my favorite people in the world. They are high school sweethearts. Well sort of. They hung out in the same tight circle with my god parents and other's that I consider aunts and uncles. My mom was smart and quiet and my dad was the handsome popular guy. He was the quarterback on the football team. The ladies loved him, including my mom. He just couldn't see it until their senior year. Mom jokes and says he got new eyes that year. She was the youngest in the crew because she skipped a grade. Her parents were throwing her a sweet sixteen and even though she had a boyfriend, dad told her that he wanted to be her escort and wasn't taking no for an answer. They'd been together ever since. She's a retired nurse and dad is a retired county worker. She had a stint with cancer when she was twenty-one, which is why she can't have kids of her own. The love those two have for each other is what people write songs about." Cooper looked up at Zolee who was sitting on the floor by her suitcase with her legs crossed.

"They set a damn good example for me."

"Sounds like a good home to grow up in. Full of love, like mine." Zolee smiled.

"Yeah. I don't want to think about where I would be if I didn't have them or if they'd given up on me when I was in what my dad calls my asshole phase."

Zolee paused holding up a pair of shorts. "Asshole phase? Oh please tell!"

Cooper stood and sat on the bench in front of the bed to be closer to Zolee. He always had this need to be no more than a few feet away from her. Zolee listened with wide eyes as he opened up about his troubled past and his issues with the law in his teens and early twenties; how he almost lost his scholarship beating the shit out of some man at a club. He told her about how he was ordered to attend therapy to manage his anger. He waited for her face to reveal any hint of judgement or fear, but all he saw was someone who was open to listening to him and empathy.

"I'm sure they are proud of you."

"Yeah, they are. Mom and Pops are my biggest fans. My dad did not want me to dance, but once he witnessed how much I loved it, he was onboard. He never questioned my sexuality or made me feel like I was less of a man for wanting to dance; never saw me as soft. What about you? I'm sure you were the perfect child."

Zolee laughed as if she was remembering something from her past. "I drove my parents crazy! I was the flighty kid that had a new dream or hobby every other month. Here were two of the most God fearing, stable, dependable people and they gave birth to a hippy who loved all things creative *and* getting high. I was a smart kid, crazy IQ but I felt that life could teach me more than school. My parents were never hard on me but I knew that I was disappointing them, so I got good grades and graduated for them. The crazy thing was I *loved* college. I thrived there because it allowed me to explore and discover my passions. I didn't feel restricted. The only thing I stayed committed to was dance and that was because my mom forced me to go when I wanted to quit. It was the best thing she could have ever done for me because I fell in love with it; allowed me to express things I couldn't with words. No dance was the same and I could be as creative as I wanted to, but even before dance I discovered that I was great with a camera. As a little kid I saw things in frames, stills, and I didn't understand why until my dad gifted me with a camera after he saw my drawings. I would draw exactly what I saw. It came natural to me so here I am, getting paid to do what I love."

Cooper smiled down at Zolee. He loved the look of passion on her face when she talked about photography. He stood and held his hand out to her.

"Come on let's get ready for bed."

After they were both showered and clothed, they snuggled up in the bed under the warm covers. Zolee tucked herself under Cooper's arm and inhaled his clean manly scent; she felt safe. Cooper gently stroked her arm with his hand, lulling her to sleep. He tried to relax but couldn't get their little spat out of his head.

"Zo."

"Mmmhmm?"

"About Sasha…"

"No Coop—"

"Let me speak Zo. You and Sasha are two different people. Actually, you two are fucking night and day. You're warm, easy going, effortlessly sexy and alluring. People don't avoid you; they are drawn to you. You don't even know the power you have."

The power you have over me, he thought.

"She's not you Zo and she doesn't come close. I don't know what is happening between us but you have nothing to worry about when it comes to Sasha. She may not give up easily but I don't want her."

I want you.

Zolee lifted up and lightly kissed Cooper on the lips. Cooper tensed at the shockwaves that flowed up his spine. A bashful grin took over her face and the room lit up.

"Thank you. Good night Coop."

Cooper took his time setting up the expresso machine to make two cups of coffee. While he preferred his black, Zolee loved hers with a third of creamer. Missy Elliot's *Rain* blasted from his phone on the counter. It was Ashli's favorite song. Cooper started the machine then placed his phone to his ear.

"What up Ash?"

"Yo! Where's my girl? You better be treating her right Coop."

"Damn so just fuck me when Zo's around."

"Don't do me like that. You know how a feel about my Coopy Coop."

"Yo, you better not say that shit around anybody."

"Especially Zo? Hmm. Where is she anyway?"

"She's in the bathroom washing up. We went for a run this morning."

"Seriously Cooper? Are you trying to kill her?"

"She's actually in pretty good shape; she kept up."

"Zo is competitive so she would have kept up if it killed her. Your relationship seems to be… umm, developing nicely." Ashli was curious about exactly what Cooper and Zo were doing. She always thought that they would be a good match which was why she invited Cooper with her to the party on Valentine's Day. They seemed to always have great times whenever they linked up since meeting but Cooper was tightlipped about his feelings and so was Zo. She was fishing for information and hoped he would take the bait.

Cooper sighed and grinned. His best friend wasn't fooling him. Ashli wanted details when it came to him and Zolee, but he didn't have any answers to give.

"It is…"

"Dammit Coop! You are my best friend and Zolee is too. What are you two doing?" Ashli whined into the phone.

"That's just it Ash. I don't know. I just know that we vibe and it feels good. We don't want to complicate things."

"You won't hurt her Coop."

"You don't know that Ash," Cooper hissed. He looked behind him to make sure Zolee was still in the bathroom. He could hear the water from the sink running and the sounds of Maxwell playing from her phone.

"You have your anger under control and Zo is easy."

"But you know I can get triggered Ash. Zo may be easy going but she's not easy."

"Ut oh. What happened?"

"Sasha happened."

"You didn't…"

"I ain't do shit Ash. I went to the store to stock the house with food and Sasha's ass showed up while I was gone. You know she was probably here talking reckless and Zo was hot! I've never seen her like that."

"Oh she really likes you!" Ashli squealed. "ZoZo ain't tripping off no bitch like Sasha unless she is really feeling you. If Sasha had tried that with Harry then she would have just shrugged it off and let her shoot her shot. Just go ahead and lock that down and make me an auntie."

Ashli mentioning Harry rubbed Cooper the wrong way, but he didn't want to give Ashli any more ammunition, so he kept quiet.

"Look I'm about to get a round in with Zo while she's still in the shower. I'll have her to call you when I'm done."

"Eww Cooper that's TMI..." Cooper chuckled, ended the call and made his way to the bathroom.

"We've got every type of sparkler you can imagine. That's about all we can do with all these damn trees around." Cooper struggled with keeping a straight face when Zolee poked out her lips and sulked. What he failed to tell her was that the community always held a huge fire work show every Fourth of July. He would make sure that they were out back facing the lake when it started. He tilted her chin up and kissed it.

"Hey, it will be fun."

"If you say so, but it won't be the same without fireworks." *Or we could make our own*, Zolee thought to herself and just like that she had an idea. Zolee loved to study all things holistic and spiritual and she wanted to try something out with Cooper.

They worked together grilling turkey burgers, kabobs, and corn on the cob. Zolee made a salad and homemade French fries. Being around each other like this felt natural for the both of them. It was effortless. Zolee hummed as she stirred the drink she'd made.

"Yo Coop, come and taste this." She handed him a glass of a beautifully made cocktail and even garnished it with a strawberry and a slice of pineapple. Cooper took a slow sip then looked up at Zolee. He flashed that devilishly handsome smile. He was pleasantly surprised.

"Damn, that's good. What is it?"

"Strawberry mango Hennessy."

"See I knew you was from the hood. This some hood shit Zo. Who makes a mix drink out of Henny, but my hood folks?"

"Whatever Coop." Zolee rolled her eyes. Cooper tilted his head back and took huge gulps from his glass. Zolee pulled the glass down away from his mouth.

"Don't drink it too fast Coop! That Henny will sneak up on you. Here drink some water. It's hot as hell outside."

Zolee maneuvered around the kitchen prepping lunch and dessert. She'd assigned Cooper to chopping any vegetables and manning the grill. While mixing the batter for her mother's famous rum pound cake Zolee kept stealing glances at Cooper. He was wearing a red, short sleeve shirt with dark wash denim shorts. His colorful tattoos were on full display. Zolee especially loved the tribal tattoo that was like a quarter sleeve. He was very purposeful in choosing the artwork that graced his body and they were all custom pieces. Cooper bit the corner of his lip as he took his time handling the knife. He was so focused on cutting the vegetables perfectly. Zolee couldn't help the giggle that escaped her mouth.

"What's so funny?" Cooper questioned.

"Nothing, just enjoying watching you in the kitchen."

Cooper nodded as he separated the finish product into separate bowls and began assembling the kabobs. He then turned his attention to Zolee.

"What's your favorite fourth of July memory?"

Zolee placed the Bundt pan in the oven then turned to face Cooper. She tried not to think of her dad as it was too painful most days, but she couldn't help the smile that crept across her face.

"I was fifteen and I wanted to spend the holiday at a pool party that all of my friends were planning on attending, but my dad wasn't having it. He said, 'Baby we got our own pool and food. You can party any other day.' He suggested that I invite my closest friends over which included Ari and a few other people. Everything was going perfect until my dad nearly burned the house down frying chicken. I guess the oil was too hot because the deep fryer erupted in flames. Instead of putting out the flames my dad ran in the house to save my mom. He runs out with her kicking and screaming about family photos and her cake in the oven. The flames then spread to the box of fireworks which set off an explosion sending me and my friends running for our dear life. Fireworks were shooting everywhere. It was like something out of a movie."

Zolee laughed as tears ran down her face and Cooper was bent over in laughter.

"Fire Rescue had to come and everything! Thank God no one got hurt but I was so embarrassed. Daddy felt terrible. Luckily, I was always good at choosing good friends; they were good sports about it. They stayed and helped clean up and we still had a great time. We ended up walking to the local park to see the fireworks."

"Damn he could have burned down the house."

"Right? My mom never let him forget it. I used to think my parents had it all together until that day. Never viewed them the same. I wish that you could have gotten to know him. He was truly the best dad; a good man."

"I'm sure he was." Cooper wrapped his arm around her shoulder and kissed Zolee on the top of her head. "Let's get this grill fired up. No pun intended."

Zolee laughed and followed him out of the kitchen.

After dinner Zolee and Cooper sat snuggled up on the lounger watching as the sun began to set over the lake. Zolee had taken a few photos and selfies. She'd even shown Cooper how to use her camera to take a few pictures of her. She wanted to remember these moments. Cooper inhaled her tropical scent and kissed her hand that was interlocked with his. She was wearing the diamond bracelets that he'd gifted her for Valentine's Day. Zolee caught Cooper off guard when she sat up and faced him.

"Hey. I want to try something with you."

Cooper's brows furrowed as she skipped to the door. "Something like what?"

"Trust me." Zolee winked before she disappeared in the house. Not even five minutes later she came back with a blanket and a cloth bag that had *Don't Stop Get It, Get It* on the front. Cooper chuckled and tugged at the handle.

"Nice bag."

"Let's go out to the dock." Cooper didn't own a boat but the house included a boat dock that was suspended across the lake. Zolee jogged ahead of Cooper and he enjoyed the view of seeing her cheeks jiggle in her short cut off shorts. She refused to wear the expected colors for the holiday and instead wore an Ankara print tube top.

"Bring your ass Coop!"

When Cooper made it to the dock, Zolee had spread the blanket across the dock. There were crystals placed evenly in a circle and something that resembled dried up grass tied together with some string. Zolee looked up at him and smiled. It made Cooper's breath hitch. She didn't just look gorgeous but she looked so peaceful and serene. He lifted her camera and snapped a couple of pictures of her. Zolee looked up at Cooper like she wanted to devour him.

"Sit." She motioned for him to sit across from her. Those words were barely above a whisper but were also so commanding that Cooper did as he was told without a slick remark.

"Okay you're pretty smart so just follow my lead." She winked and flashed a scheming grin.

Zolee locked hands with Cooper then locked eyes with him. She instructed him to take deep breaths with her. They took several deep breaths as they stared into each other's eyes. The experience was uncomfortable at first but the more they breathed the more they relaxed. Next, Zolee place one hand near her heart and the other near Cooper's and he mimicked her actions. As they felt each other's heart beat their breathing eventually fell in sync with each other. Zolee shivered as her skin prickled with goosebumps. She then sat up on her knees and moved closer to Cooper. Her hands caressed his face and slowly moved down his neck. She tugged at the hem of his shirt and he lifted his arms to assist her in removing it.

"Touch me," she spoke softly and full of vulnerability.

Cooper's fingers ran down Zolee's arm. When his rough fingers grazed down Zolee's ribs she jumped and her breathing picked up. A moan escaped her mouth when he massaged her thigh. She let him take the lead and began to mimic his movements. As the summer sun began to set Cooper and Zolee explored each other's bodies with just the touch of their hands.

Zolee leaned into Cooper and let her lips softly brush against his. She smiled as she teased his lips with her tongue before she allowed his to slip into her mouth. Their kisses held a hint of henny and strawberries. As their tongues dance around each other Cooper slid Zolee's top down to her waist. He wasted no time cupping her breast with his hands. He dipped his head down and took in her left nipple into his mouth because he knew it was more sensitive than the other.

"Mmm Coop." Zolee's body was on fire and she couldn't take it anymore. She began to unbuckle Cooper's shorts. He stood up and let them fall to the dock before he stepped out of them and Zolee did the same with her top, shorts, and panties. Cooper's eyes darkened as he closed the space between the two of them and wrapped his arm around her. He laid her down on the blanket and explored her entire body with his lips. His body was humming with need. All he knew was that he'd never felt this open and this aware to what his body was feeling. When he hooked Zolee's legs into the crook of his arms and entered her they both released a guttural moan. Cooper would normally try to pace himself but his body was sensitive to every feeling and touch. Zolee's body wrapped all around him felt too good. He bit down on his bottom lip to keep from fully verbalizing his pleasure but a growl escaped his mouth.

"Shhiiit Zo. You feel so damn good."

He slowly moved in and out of Zolee with perfect precision. The steady pattern of his movements drove Zolee wild. She felt him all over as his hardness massaged her warm walls. The pleasurable feeling that he was providing was too much for her. Before she realized what was happening her stomach tighten and quickly released as she was hit with continuous shocks of pleasure. She moaned and whimpered as Cooper flung his head back and released into her while spewing profanities. The sky illuminated with the first burst of colorful fireworks over the lake. Cooper collapsed next to Zolee as they looked up at the sky. Zolee felt like the colors were raining on them.

"What the fuck did you do Zo?"

"Zolee shrugged and sat up. Been studying tantra and tantric sex, but damn. I had no idea."

Zolee reached into her bag of tricks and pulled out the sparklers. She lit two and danced around the dock naked. Cooper snapped a few more pictures before he sat the camera down. He selected a station from his music app and slipped on his boxers. He danced with Zolee on the dock as she twirled and laughed. Zolee stopped to catch her breath. What she and Cooper had just shared and experienced was beyond just sexual, it was spiritual, soulful. She'd always felt a certain connection with Cooper from the day they met but this was something different. Their souls were bound. It felt like their spirits recognized each other from a past life. They saw the best and some of the worst of each other. It felt a lot like *love*. The pleading look in Zolee's eyes alarmed Cooper.

"Hey, what's wrong?"

Zolee sucked in her bottom lip then ran her hands up his chest. "I don't want you to see anyone else."

Cooper smirked and flashed those dimples. He brushed his nose against hers. "After what I just experience, that shit you just put on me, you can have whatever you want ZoZo baby." Cooper was so far gone off of what they'd just shared that Zolee could have anything she wanted at this point. She was fucking magic.

Fall

Chapter 8

Cooper stared at the email and couldn't believe that he'd did it. After linking up with a private investigator he'd located his mother and biological family. Rolanda Moore, daughter of Roland and Wanda Moore, she was the youngest of six. Six aunts and uncles which could mean a ton of cousins and possibly other siblings. She lived about thirty minutes across town in Riverdale. She was a hair stylist and worked at a neighborhood salon.

"Earth to Cooper..."

"Huh?" He looked up from his phone and couldn't fight the smile that formed on his face and the flutters in his stomach if he wanted to. This woman made Cooper feel like a teenage boy with a crush. Zolee stood in front of him wrapped up in white satin sheets, her locs wild and all over her head. Cooper thought she looked absolutely heavenly. He dropped his phone and pulled her to stand in between his legs. Zolee placed her hands on his shoulders and stared into his eyes. She seem so comfortable in his space, so at peace.

They'd hit a few bumps in the road the following months after the Fourth. Copper attributed to the huge gap between then and their next scheduled visit. They'd had a couple of fights over dumb shit. The last argument they had was over pictures that popped up on social media with him out with Queen. They'd had a long practice and she invited him to a late dinner. Well, paparazzi took several pictures and spun their relationship into something it definitely wasn't. He hadn't been on any of his accounts and only found out because Zolee texted him the pictures. He'd tried to call after that but she ignored him for over a week and when she did finally answer she was extremely difficult. She triggered something in him and he ended up snapping on her and hanging up. The next couple of weeks after that were unbearable for both of them. Cooper broke the ice by purchasing her plane ticket for November. She called him as soon as she got the confirmation email. Cooper apologized as soon as he answered the call and she followed up with one herself. Although they'd apologize they never discussed the actual fight. He didn't like being at odds with Zolee and preferred to move on from it.

"A penny for your thoughts?" She massaged his shoulders. He pulled her closer and wrapped his arms around her.

"It's nothing major. I was just going through my emails." Cooper shook his head. He unwrapped the sheets and began planting kisses on Zolee's stomach. Her breath hitched and she panted. Her hands rubbed his head then gripped his ears. His hands caressed and massaged her thighs before he inserted two fingers into her nectar. Zolee moaned and opened her legs more to give him access. When he curved his index finger and rubbed her spot, she gasped then flung her head back. Cooper had been the only man to leave her so open and vulnerable. She was at his mercy whenever they were intimate.

"Ah shit Coop. Yes. Yes!"

She rode his fingers and she quickly unraveled. Zolee whimpered and moaned at the delicious pleasure that Cooper was giving her.

"That's right Zo. Give it all to me." Zolee tried to pull away but Cooper wouldn't budge and continued to massage her love button with his finger and the wetter she got the better it felt. It felt too damn good. This feeling can't be normal.

"Coop I can't…"

"You will. Just one more." They went at it for hours the night before when she arrived but Cooper relished in witnessing Zolee's orgasms; the pure bliss on her face. He wrapped one arm around her and moved them down on the floor. His finger remained working her middle as he let his tongue work her clit. Zolee clawed at the floor and screamed. She lifted up as if she was possessed. Her beautiful body convulsed as wave after wave of pleasure entered and exited her body. This was Cooper's favorite part. The shit turned him on. He kissed up her body until they were mouth to mouth and their tongues tangled together.

"See how fucking sweet you are?"

"Mmhm..." Zolee's body went limp and he scooped her up.

"Come on, let's clean up."

Knowing that he was going to be late he should have opted for the shower, but Cooper had worked Zolee's body over and he knew she needed to soak so he ran water in the tub. They took turns bathing each other, both with silly grins on their faces.

Zolee enjoyed watching Cooper in his element. Today he was overseeing the rehearsal for Young Troy's BET Awards perform-ance and he'd let her tag along. Although she knew that Young Troy was an ass Zolee was still star struck when he decided to introduce himself to her. Cooper was focused working with a group of kids who were excited about the opportunity to be on TV. They were a ball of energy but they soaked in everything that Cooper said to them. Zolee smiled as she watched him do his thing along with Ari and Ashli. Ari flew down with Zolee on a whim and Ash was in town for the holiday. Neither of them would be there for Thanksgiving dinner since they had plans to spend it with their family, well Ari was invited to spend the holiday with Brandon's sister.

"Hey Mr. Coop. Is that your girlfriend that came in with you?"

"Cooper glanced over at Zolee with a salacious smile on his face that had her squirming in her seat."

"She's a very special friend." He signaled for Zolee to come over with his head and she hesitantly stood up. He pulled her in front of him when she stood by his side.

"Guys this is Ms. Zolee. Say hi."

"Hi Ms. Zolee!"

"Hey everyone. You all have been doing an amazing job!"

"What you all don't know is that Ms. Zolee is a dancer."

"Oh word? Well show us what you got Ms. Zolee." Young Troy moved to stand a little too close to Zolee. She turned to him and smiled. Zolee waved her hands and stepped back.

"No, I couldn't you guys are busy."

"Nah sweetie, I pay the bills here so what I say goes." Cooper clinched his fists when Troy placed his hand at the small of Zolee's back.

"Well if the boss is asking who am I to say no?" Cooper bristled at her response and tried to brush it off. He stepped back and allowed Zolee to do her thing. Cooper couldn't lie, he was impressed. Zolee was an amazing dancer; a natural. For her to be so indifferent about kids she was great with them and they took to her fairly quickly.

Young Troy played around Zolee as if he was trying to learn the moves. He was able to pull a couple of laughs out of Zo. Zolee knew he wasn't shit, but he was funny so she would play nice. Cooper walked over to Ashli and Ari. Ashli watched him. She noticed that his body was tensed and was concerned.

"Hey Coop. Are you good?"

Cooper shook his head and drank from his water bottle. "This bitch ass nigga was just flirting with Zo to get to me and she's fucking oblivious." Cooper was angry with himself for bringing her around. Troy was a womanizer and preyed on women. He was the type to promise women the world only to use them up and toss them away. Just like he did Sasha. He'd reluctantly let her take over the rehearsal and in Zolee fashion she'd effortlessly won everyone over, but this was his rehearsal, his dancers, his job. When Troy leaned down and whispered in Zo's ear that was it for Coop.

"I'm over this shit." Cooper mumbled as he walked back towards Zolee. Ashli called his name but he kept moving forward. He couldn't fight the anger that was bubbling over. Cooper wanted to snatch Zo out of his reach and repeatedly punch Young Troy's face in. She was *his*. Cooper's whole body stiffened when Zolee placed her small hands on his arm.

"Did you hear what Troy said? Looks like I'm going on tour with you Mr. Big Shot." Zolee had fun and was excited to experience working with a celebrity even if he was a slimy jerk. Cooper hadn't heard what that lame said due to the ringing in his ears.

"Maybe you and Ashli can split this with me and make this partnership a trio." Zolee poked Cooper in the ribs a couple of times.

"Will you just STOP!" Copper yelled and the entire room fell quiet. Zolee's neck rolled as she looked Cooper up and down. She thought he must have lost his mind.

"What the hell is up with you?"

"YOU! You... you're... You're just too much Zo! *This* is too damn much..." As soon as those words left his mouth and Zolee's face fell he immediately regretted it. Zolee blinked but then scoffed as she walked past him without a word.

"Zo wait. I didn't mean... Zo! Zolee!" Cooper started after her but Ari and Ashli blocked Cooper from following behind her.

Cooper kissed his teeth. "Man y'all move."

"No you need to cool down," Ashli spoke in a hushed tone.

"What did you do? What did you say to her?" Ari questioned.

Cooper sighed and snatched his cap off his head.

"I told her that she was too much."

"YOU DID WHAT?!" Ashli and Ari both yelled in unison. Ari approached Cooper like she was ready to whip his ass as her nose flared and her brows furrowed. Ashli extended her arm to keep them separated.

"Coop why would you say that?" Ashli looked at Cooper in disappointment and he knew he had messed up.

"Those were the exact words her ex-boyfriend used on her you asshole! I can't believe you! You need to fix this!" Ari yelled and pointed her finger in his face while people looked on. Cooper stuffed his hands in his pockets and rocked on his heels to remain calm.

"Look we not doing that shit in here so calm your ass down Ari. I am working right now. I'll link up with Zo later and smooth things out okay?"

"Hmph, you better."

Although there was confidence in his words, Cooper wasn't sure where he stood with Zo at this point. The way she looked at him made him uneasy.

Ari: Zo answer this damn phone!

Zolee glanced at her phone then slid it across the floor. She found herself back at Coop's place packing her suitcase but she couldn't gather the nerve to finish. Although she was hurt she didn't want to leave so she found herself on the floor in his room rocking back and forth. His hurtful words immediately pulled her back to a place she didn't want to ever be in. Zolee felt like she was regressing, falling into sadness and eventually depression. Zolee tried to tune out the negative thoughts that no man would ever love her, that she wasn't worth love, that she was a burden, that she wasn't enough and, that no one would miss her if she was gone.

"Just shut up please!" Zolee sobbed and pulled at her hair with both fists.

"Hello? Is someone here?"

Zolee jumped but didn't have the energy to get up when an older couple that she knew to be Cooper's parents walked into the room. They looked down at her with concern and confusion. She figured that she had to look crazy to them. A strange woman in their son's room, on the floor, talking to herself and crying. His father spoke first.

"Young lady are you okay? Where's my son?" Zolee couldn't help herself but she scoffed and rolled her eyes.

"Um Matthew can you go put up the food except for the Turkey?"

"Ah yeah, okay, sure." Cooper's dad gave Zolee one last worried glance before exiting Cooper's room.

To Zolee's surprise his mother sat next to her on the floor and pulled her into her arms. Lela had experienced seeing people come into the emergency room in a similar state, so she understood how fragile she probably was even if she didn't know why.

Touched by the compassion of a stranger, Zolee held her tight and cried until her body relaxed and her anxiety subsided. His mom held her at arm's length and smiled.

"Zolee I presume?"

"Yes. I'm pleased to meet you. Sorry you had to see me like that."

"Honey are you okay?"

"Honestly, I don't know. Something was said that triggered me."

"Was it something Coop said?" Zolee shook her head ready to lie but his mom held up her hand."

"Don't do that. Do you want to know the best way to get on my good side? Don't lie to me young lady. I know my son and I know his temperament."

Zolee fidgeted with her hands and hesitated. Lela chuckled.

"You don't have to tell me what he said. Like I stated, I *know* my son. He's a good man you know. He just tends to let his emotions take over him and ends up putting his foot in his big mouth. My son has been searching for love and acceptance all his life to make up for his parents and biological family abandoning him. He chased it in women, work, partying, whatever thing that would keep him occupied, but all he had to do was accept that our love, mine and his father's love, was enough. Cooper talks about you a lot and I am all too familiar with the look on his face when he does. My son is smitten with you.

"I have an idea why you too are at odds. My son struggles with accepting the love of others when his own parents didn't love him enough. He doesn't understand it and he will fight against it. The thing is he is so loving and charismatic that everyone who gets to know him loves him and he's very territorial of the people he cares about."

Zolee wiped her eyes and laughed.

"I can definitely see *that*. I haven't celebrated holidays in three years and because of him I've acknowledged or celebrated every holiday this year. He didn't even know me and was invested in my happiness but today he... I- I don't know, I guess I just saw a side of him I didn't like; a side I didn't recognize."

His mom nodded and patted Zolee's thigh.

"You don't think my friends and my husband have sides of them that I don't like? He may seem perfect to you now, but he is a man, a flawed man. Get Cooper off that pedestal Zolee or you will forever be disappointed." Zolee didn't respond but held on to her words. Lela released a sigh and patted Zolee on her thigh again.

"We've just met, but I need to ask you a favor."

"Yeah sure, what is it?"

"Cooper is planning to sneak and see his mom early in the morning. He doesn't know that I know but I overheard him on the phone with his cousin Deacon. I need you to go with him. It's not going to be good and he's not going to get the reunion he's hoping for. His biological mother? That woman is something else."

Zolee pulled at one of her locs and looked ahead. "I don't know Mrs. Powers. We just had a fight and I'm not even sure if I want to stay. How am I supposed to bring it up?"

"Child just tell him that I told you. I don't care if he knows. I am the parent baby."

Zolee thought about what she was being asked to do. Although she decided that she would leave she didn't want Cooper to see his biological mom for the first time by himself. He needed a friend and she would be just that.

"Okay. Yes mam. I'm still mad at him, but I'll be there to support him."

"Thank you. Now I'm not leaving you in here alone to stew in a cloud of darkness. Come on and help me prep this food."

"I would love that. Let me wash up and I'll be right there."

Helping Cooper's mom prepare for tomorrow's dinner was nostalgic for Zolee. It brought back memories of her helping her mom in the kitchen while her dad fried the turkey outside. They played music and chatted while they got everything prep to cook in the morning.

When Cooper walked in, he released a sigh of relief when he realized that Zolee hadn't left. He worried that she would leave and left the studio early to catch her. Zolee acknowledged him with a simple head nod and she finished making the stuffing. Cooper stepped into the kitchen, threaded his hand through her locs and kissed the side of her head before he greeted his mom with a tight embrace.

"Hey mom. So, you've met my ZoZo." She tried to hide it, but he saw Zolee blush.

"I have." She gave Cooper a look that only a mother could give which let him know that she and Zolee had been talking. He whispered in her ear.

"I'm going to fix it ma." She didn't respond but simply nodded her head full of long salt and pepper twists before giving him instructions.

"Well go wash your hands and help your dad with seasoning all that meat."

Cooper tilted his chin up at his father. "What up dad?"

"Hey son, about time you acknowledge your old man. Giving the women all your attention when they ain't nothing but headaches."

"You watch your mouth old man!" Lela shook her spoon at Matthew. Cooper's dad laughed before he stood and planted a kiss on his wife's lips. Zolee placed the stuffing mix into the refrigerator then gazed upon his parents and their antics; she smiled. Cooper's attention was on Zolee. When their eyes connected, Zolee's eyes narrowed before she stormed off to the living room. Cooper could have sworn she rolled her eyes. This was going to be a long holiday.

The next morning Cooper quietly eased out of bed, but when he stood up and turned around, he realized that Zolee was gone.

"Dammit Zo." Cooper's heart rate sped up as he spun around the room and looked for any traces that she was still there. The first thought that had come to mind was that she left him, and his body stiffened with anger. He rubbed his hands down his face and took a cleansing breath. Cooper's head shot up when the doorknob to his room slowly turned and Zolee stepped in.

"Oh! You're up."

Cooper's shoulders dropped as he released a sigh of relief. He thought that she was gone, that she'd left him. He didn't like the uncertainty in her eyes. She was being cautious of how she interacted with him.

"Coop are you okay?"

"Ah, yeah. What are you doing up?"

"Same reason you're up. I'm going with you." Zolee closed the door and pressed her back against it.

"Nah, you don't have to do that." Cooper shook his head. "And how the hell did you know?"

"You can't get anything past a black mother Coop. Now hurry up your mom will have your ass and mine if we're late for dinner. I made us coffee. I'll be outside on the porch waiting for you."

Zolee smiled but it didn't reach those beautiful dark eyes. She wasn't her normal upbeat self and that bothered Cooper. He was hoping they would start new in the morning, but she was obviously still salty from his outburst. Cooper shook the thoughts away and focused on getting ready to visit the woman who gave birth to him.

Thirty minutes later they pulled up to a moderate size brickhouse. The yard was neatly manicured and there was a beautiful magnolia tree in the middle of the yard. Cooper and Zolee sat in the car listening to the music play from the radio. Cooper nervously tapped the steering wheel. To Zolee he looked like a scared little boy and it tugged at her heart strings. She unhooked her seat belt then reached for his hand and squeezed it.

"Come on. Let's do this." Cooper looked at Zolee and sighed in relief. He didn't want to do it alone and was appreciative that Zolee offered. He turned off the car and made his exit. He opened Zolee's door and helped her out of the vehicle. Before they could make it up the porch the door swung open.

"Oh! Oh, Jesus you almost gave me a heart attack..." The woman's words faded when her eyes left Zolee's and landed on Cooper's.

"We're sorry mam but are you Rolanda Moore?"

"No, I'm not."

"Um, okay. Does she live here?"

"No, she doesn't." Both Cooper and Zolee stared at her in disbelief. The woman in front of them looked like Cooper. He obviously got his skin tone, eye color, mouth, and dimples from her. When she raised her chin in defiance Zolee spoke.

"Let's go. I think you got your answer." Zolee wasn't going to stand here and let this lady continue to deny Cooper and hurt him even more than she already had. She was upset with him but felt protective of him in this vulnerable moment. Cooper's mom spoke when they were halfway down the sidewalk.

"I know why you're here. I know who you are." Cooper stopped in his tracks but didn't turn around.

"The anger, the quick temper, the blind rage. Does that sound familiar? Hmph you don't have to answer, it is radiating all over you. You get *that* from your damn daddy, which is why I never wanted you. I used to pray to God for a miscarriage when I found out that I was carrying a boy. I didn't need another man to abuse me or any other woman for that matter."

Rolanda stepped off the porch and approached them. Cooper swallowed the lump that formed in his throat, shocked at what she was saying. He faced her and gently pushed Zolee back. She looked around Cooper and set her sights on Zolee. "Little girl you should run while you have a chance. He's got the devil in him just like his father. I should have had you at home and threw you in the river! Evil! EVIL!"

Cooper cringed every time she yelled those cruel words; felt like being slapped. He was stunned into silence. His heart pounded so hard and fast that it hurt. Cooper took deep breaths to tame the rage that was slowly rising, the rage he'd worked so hard to bury. He felt a hand softly push against his chest until he stepped back.

"How dare you talk to him like that? You don't know a damn thing about him, but we know that you ain't shit! You ain't nothing but a trifling, poor excuse for a woman! Your son..." Zolee choked on her words. "He's a good, successful man no thanks to you. He's gentle and sweet and loving; no thanks to you. Coop is better off. Fuck you!" Zolee jumped at her which forced Rolanda to stumble backwards. Cooper tightly wrapped his arms around her waist and dragged her away. When they reached his car, he pulled her in a hug and broke down. Cooper's body trembled against hers. His cries broke Zolee's heart and pissed her off at the same time. His tears trickled down her neck and she allowed her own to fall. Cooper tried to pull away, but Zolee held him tighter and stroked her hand up and down his back.

She whispered into his ear, "You're going to let all this out and let this go before we get in the car. Leave it here."

"Why does she hate me so much? Why didn't she want me?" Cooper mumbled through his sobs.

"That woman is not your mother, Ms. Lela is. *They* love you Coop. Your friends love you. The Powers adopted you and gave you their last name. You are loved so much. Matthew and Lela chose you. They wanted you. You *are* wanted. You are enough. That's some special shit."

Zolee held Cooper by his face and lifted his head until their eyes met. Her soft plumped lips pressed into his, but not long enough for Cooper. Something else was definitely up with Zo. He didn't have the energy to address it and would accept her support for now. He helped Zolee into his car and closed her door. He took a minute to gather himself before he made it in on his side. Cooper powered up the car, pulled out of the parking space and didn't think of looking back. There was nothing there for him; he was starting to realize that he had everything he needed.

Despite the rocky morning Thanksgiving was great. Cooper was proud to have Zolee seated next to him. She'd already won over his mom and dad and his cousin Deacon was warming up to her rather quickly. He was pleased that she was having a great time. The thing was she was laughing and talking to everyone but him. She would give him a few quick glances to check if he was okay, but that was it. They needed to talk but he would wait until after dinner and the game. To his surprise Zolee watched the game with them and talked more shit than Deacon and his dad. The Atlanta Hawks were playing the Magic City Thunder which was Zo's home team. Unfortunately for him, MCT won, but

Cooper was satisfied that he got to enjoy Zolee's little victory dance. Cooper was hoping that she would show him that dance again alone in his bedroom tonight. He was glad that his parents were going back home. Since they'd slept over the night before he could not have Zolee like he wanted too.

He stood up and motioned for Zolee to follow him. "Hey, let's pack up so we can go to Lake Lanier tomorrow. When my parents leave, we can head out and I can have that ass all to myself. Strangely, seeing you all hyped up about that game turned me on."

Zolee followed but didn't speak until they were in the privacy of his bedroom. "Um I don't think that's a good idea." Cooper frowned and crossed his arms over his chest.

"What do you mean?"

"I mean... I moved up my flight Coop. We need some time apart. I am leaving tomorrow."

"Tomorrow? You're supposed to fly out on Sunday evening. What the hell is this about? Are you still upset about what happened at the rehearsal?"

"Am I still upset that you completely spazzed out on me in front of my friends and all those strangers and haven't apologized? Hell yeah I am pissed Cooper." Zolee's voice was low but her tone and body language told how upset she was.

Cooper massaged his temples. Zo was always so easygoing and cool that he didn't understand why she was still upset with him. She had erected a wall and was doing everything to keep him out. He could feel the separation.

"I can't keep tiptoeing around your emotions."

"Who asked you to do that because I sure as hell didn't. You don't have to tip toe around shit, but you will respect me."

"Now I don't respect you? Come on Zo what is this about?"

"It's about us needing space. This was supposed to be fun not us arguing."

"We're people Zo, people argue."

"This was supposed to be different Cooper." Zolee continued flinging items into her suitcase.

"Zo stop. Please." Cooper didn't like the look of finality on her face. He couldn't let her leave like that. It didn't feel right. Cooper attempted to pull Zolee closer, but she stepped back and held her hands up.

"Our friends told you why your outburst hurt me and you haven't said shit! That shit didn't just hurt me, it triggered me. It brought up emotions that I never wanted to feel again and just like before I had to deal with them alone! I refused to let anyone push me back into that dark space."

"Zo, I wasn't purposefully avoiding that conversation. I was about to meet my *mother*. Obviously, I had other shit on my mind."

"Exactly and that *bitch* ain't your mother! Don't disrespect Ms. Lela like that."

"You're being a brat right now."

"Don't talk to me that way!"

Cooper looked up, surprised by her reaction. Zolee's nose flared and her chest was heaving up and down. "What are you talking about? I've called to a brat before."

"Not like this. Your tone is teetering on disrespectful. My dad would *never* talk to me..."

"HE AIN'T HERE!" Cooper snapped.

"Woah. Wow. How could you say that?" The expression on Zolee's face was pained.

"Shit, baby I didn't mean that." He moved closer to Zolee, but she stepped out of his reach.

"You tend to say some really hurtful things when you're upset Cooper. I can't. How could you? No, I should go. Yeah. I think that's best."

"Zo please."

Zolee's shoulders slumped; she felt defeated. "Just let me go home. I have a car that should be here shortly. I reserved a room at a hotel near the airport. I'll text you when I get in safe." She sniffed but held it together.

Zolee left out of the room without another word. Cooper sat on the bed and tried to figure out how things went left with them. He'd fucked up. Five minutes later he heard voices saying goodbye and the front door closing shut.

Chapter 9

I t didn't feel right and Zolee was unsettled about it. She hadn't talked to Cooper in over a week and that wasn't for his lack of trying. Cooper called, texted, and made attempts to face-time her but Zolee felt like they needed space, she needed space. After their little turkey day spat, she realized how much Cooper could hurt her if things didn't work out between the two of them. He had the power to break her heart and she refused to go through that pain again. Something told her that this time around would be worse, and she had to protect her heart, hell her sanity. Zolee held up her dad's blue Hawaiian print shirt and grinned.

"Ma, is this the...?"

"The infamous Fourth of July fire shirt? It sure is. That man nearly gave me a heart attack and scared your little friends half to death!"

"He sure did." Zolee carefully folded the shirt and held it to her chest. She sniffed the shirt and sighed. "Do you mind if I keep it mom?"

"No go ahead." Zora watched her daughter as she placed the shirt on top of her purse among other little items she'd asked to have like his pocket watch and harmonica. She was concerned if Zolee was ready for this. "Baby, are you sure that you are okay with this?"

Zolee and her mom were sorting through her father's belongings. Her mom had finally made the decision to clear out his side of the closet and the attic with Zolee's support. There was a pile to donate, a pile to keep and a pile to throw away. In the past she'd been a brat about her mom giving away her father's belongings and lashed out at her whenever she would broach the subject. Zolee now felt strong enough to part with them; it was time.

"Yes, I'm fine. It's time."

Zora twisted up her mouth and crossed her arms. "Then why are you over there moping with your lip poked out like someone shot your puppy?" Zolee balled up her face at the analogy and shook her head. She then released a sigh and plopped down on her mom's bed. Her chest tightened whenever she thought about their last interaction.

"It's Coop. We sort of had a fight. Mom he just lost it and went off on me over something that was so minor. It made me realize that I don't really know him."

"Well of course you don't know him! You've known each other for about nine months Zo. Now don't look at me like that. I'm not saying that it's a bad thing, but in this season of getting to know each other you will learn more things about him and you won't necessarily like all of it. That's how relationships are. You should be asking yourself what you are not willing to deal with."

"But he can't speak to me the way he did mom."

"Then tell him that baby. Don't shut him out. You may miss out on the love of a lifetime."

"Who said anything about love?" Zolee rolled her eyes and started shoving items in boxes.

"Little girl please do not insult me. You and Cooper have known each other long enough and if you haven't fallen in love yet then you are just wasting time."

"I don't want to talk about this anymore." Zolee huffed then plopped back down on the bed. Her mother scoffed.

"Fine, have ya little attitude. You can be so damn stubborn sometimes. You get that from your daddy. Just take some time to think about it before you burn any bridges." Zora snatched Zolee up in a hug and sighed. "I love you. Don't shut yourself off from love because you are afraid of getting your heart broken. Lorenz was never the man for you. This thing that you have with Cooper is special. I've seen the way that man looks at you. Now help me clean up in here. The veteran's truck will be here first thing in the morning to get the donations."

Zolee smiled and wrapped her arms around her mom. "I love you. Thanks mom."

"Hey my beautiful, bossy, badass queens! Today I will be unboxing a package that I received from Dahlia Beauty. Dahlia Beauty specializes in natural skin care products and it is... drumroll please. Black owned! Yessss! Now y'all know how much I love and support my melanated boss babes. So, I've already gotten the box that it was shipped in opened up and let me tell you, this company knows how to select beautiful packaging. Look at this box! I love that the colors are gold and lilac. It just screams regal."

Zolee opened the box and made sure to hold it at the best angle possible. The jar labeled *Oatmeal Cookie Surprise* immediately caught her attention, so she pulled it out as she spoke to the camera and showed off the cute jar. She carefully opened it and took a quick whiff.

"Oh my God Queens I wish you could smell this. It smells so good and sexy. Just like a cookie. This will have the men or ladies wanting to eat you up!"

Zolee bit her lip then winked at the camera. She scooped up the creamy body butter with her middle finger and rubbed it on her hand then raved about how good it felt. It left her skin glowing. When Zolee was done with all of the products she shared how to follow Dahlia Beauty and where to purchase the products. She then changed her top and make-up before doing two more unboxings. By the time she wrapped up the last video she was starving. She would do her edits in the morning. Remembering that she had left-over roasted chicken from the other night Zolee decided to make a salad with it. Before digging in she snapped a quick photo of her meal and posted on her social media with the hashtag *healthy food ain't boring*. Ro James blasted from her phone startling her. It was Coop's ringtone. She quickly silenced her phone then stabbed at her salad. After she was full and had the kitchen cleaned up Zolee's phone rang again but this time it was Ashli.

"Hey hun!"

"Zolee muthafuckin' Rose Norwood! What the hell?"

Ashli was practically screaming so Zolee pulled the phone away from her ear and pressed the speaker button.

"If you don't stop yelling, I will hang up on your ass Ash."

"Why won't you answer his calls Zo? That is so immature."

Of course this was about Coop. Zolee kissed her teeth as she abandoned her salad and started to reorganize her workspace.

"You were there. Did you forget what he did? Did he ask you to call? I know that's your real best friend but…"

"But nothing Zo. Coop was dead ass wrong for what he said and how he behaved. You've expressed that to him. I've expressed that to him and so did Arianne. He is sorry Zo. He feels like shit. Cooper is complicated and like you, he has things that he's working on. We all have flaws. If you keep this up, you will be alone forever!" That hit a nerve. Ashli made it sound like it was Zolee's own fault that she was single. It took months of therapy for her to stop blaming herself for her failed relationship and she did not want to do that shit again.

"How about you just mind your business and respect my decision Ashli. Coop and I are grown. He needs to respect that I need space and so do you. This don't have shit to do with you so if you didn't call for anything else then…"

"Kiss my ass Zo. I hope you figure out what the hell you want soon because we will *all* be in Southwest Florida for Christmas in that Airbnb we rented. Bet your ass forgot about that!" Before Zolee could respond the line went dead.

"Shit, shit, shit!" Zolee kicked and punched at the air like a ninja while she worked through her tantrum.

"Dammit!"

There was a knock at the door. Zolee stomped to the door while trying to catch her breath. She assumed it was Ari coming over to give her more grief over Coop, so she flung the door open.

"I don't want to hear it!"

"Hear what?"

"Harry? How did you get up here?" Zolee gave Harry the once

over. He looked good in his green long sleeved crewneck sweater with dark jeans. He reminded her of a young Michael Ely and he smelled good.

"Somebody was exiting as I was walking up and held the door open for me. Are you going to invite me in?"

Zolee really wanted to tell him *hell no*, since he showed up unannounced, but he looked so damn pitiful and handsome. She stepped aside and signaled for him to enter.

"No more pop ups Harry. You need to call next time," she warned.

He swaggered in and took a seat on the couch. Zolee followed and Harry's eyes roamed over her body and lingered at her legs. He loved the way her lower half looked in tights and he wanted nothing more than to rip them off of her. He tried to pull her between his legs but Zolee side stepped him and sat next to him. She tucked one of her legs under her.

"Where have you been Zoe?"

"What do you mean where have I been? I've been working, doing me."

"I mean why haven't I seen you? You ignore my calls, you barely answer my texts, and when I try to spend time with you, you always have an excuse. I know you are a free spirit, but you use to at least check in with me. Are you seeing someone else?"

"Does it matter? We were not exclusive Harry." Zolee shrugged and picked at one of her nails.

"Can you just answer the damn question and stop asking questions in return?" Zolee bit her tongue and scooted away from Harry. She shook her head and released a dark chuckle. She was not about to do this again, especially not with him.

"You don't get to question me Harry, but I should make things clear. Like I stated, we are not exclusive Harry. So yes, I have been seeing someone else. Yes, he is the reason why you couldn't keep my attention; he's has it." Zolee's eyes stung with tears that she quickly blinked away.

"Yeah, I know that shit."

"Excuse you?"

"Yeah I called you on Easter. My family was having their annual cookout and I wanted to invite you. Some thug picked up the phone talking about you were busy and I could talk to you when he was done. Is that the type of man you want Lee?"

Dammit Coop. Zolee couldn't believe that he would do something like that. She was pissed that he would cross the line and answer her phone but the thought that he felt the need to do that made her smile.

"Seriously Zo? You think that shit is cute?"

"No I think Cooper is cute. That's his name and he's not some thug. You know what?" Zolee stood up and walked closer to the door.

"I like you Harry. I think you are good people, but the romantic chemistry is just not there. I don't want to pursue a relationship with you and I don't want to date you anymore."

Harry held his head down in defeat. "This would be easier to take if you'd actually given me a chance and put effort into dating me. You had a wall up the entire time Zolee. You weren't that free-spirited woman I met at the photoshoot. I thought maybe you hadn't dated in a while, so I was patient with you. You were always so closed off and maybe I should have taken that as a sign. You telling me the name of this guy you're seeing is the most personal information you've shared. He must have found the secret to break through that tough armor."

Harry looked crushed which caused Zolee's face to fall. She hadn't realized how much he liked her and she hadn't realized that she'd blocked him out. She thought that they were just having fun.

"Harry I'm sorry. We should have had this conversation a while ago. I do want to be your friend if you don't hate me."

Harry stood from the couch and made his way to her. He tugged at the hem of her Angela Davis cropped top. "I can't hate you Lee but I don't think I can be your friend. At least not right now."

"I respect that but remember that we run in the same circle so we will see each other. When that happens, I don't want it to be awkward."

"It won't be, I promise." Harry pulled Zolee into a quick hug before he allowed her to escort him to the door.

"Oh and Harry?"

"Yeah?"

"Don't get in the habit of calling me Lee. My ex-fiancé use to call me that and I hate it."

"Noted. Now see, was opening up about that so hard?" He chuckled.

Zolee smiled and rubbed her arm.

"No, it wasn't. You take care Harry."

"You too. See you around."

Zolee locked the door behind Harry and sighed. She missed Cooper terribly.

"What the hell am I doing?"

****

"This girl looks flawless. She almost makes me regret choosing her. Shit!"

"What's that?"

Cooper had just wrapped up rehearsing with Queen. She had the choreography down so now they were working on her adding her own flavor to it to make it look natural and seamless. While he was cleaning up, she was focused on her phone.

"The ambassadors for my intimates line was just revealed on all social media platforms and this girl stole the entire show and made it hers. Here, take a look." Queen knew the first few pictures were of her then group shots. She wanted Cooper to see what she looked like with as little clothes on as possible. She was so sure that she would have had him in her bed by now, but he would not take the bait; he was different. He swiped through and didn't even react to her pictures. Queen frowned when she noticed a spark in his eyes.

"Zolee," Cooper whispered and his eyes brightened. Queen raised her eyebrows.

"You know her?"

"Yeah I do. Damn she looks amazing."

"Oh you know her, know her." She carefully tugged her phone

out of Cooper's grasp.

"Queenie..."

"What? Damn with the way you are looking at her I definitely don't have a shot."

Cooper finally glanced back up at Queen and gave her a sympathetic smile.

"Yeah, sorry. She fucking frustrates me but- but that's my baby. She has my heart."

"Wow, why do I get the feeling that there is trouble in paradise? What did you do? I didn't take you for a jerk..."

"I'm not but I was a complete jerk towards her. I apologized but my actions affected her deeper than I could fathom." Cooper couldn't not believe that he was having this conversation with Queen, but she'd always been cool and her flirting was always innocent. She'd never crossed the line.

"Okay and?" Cooper looked at her and shrugged before he continued to clean up the room. Queen strutted over to him and stood in his way.

"What are you going to do about it? If you just let her go that easily then you are both stupid and a jerk. Dude! You saw her pictures and I've met her. The girl is beautiful and she has a bomb personality. How long do you think it would take for someone else to snatch her up?"

"Damn you must didn't like me as much as you thought you did. I would think you would be trying to shoot your shot." She held her hands up and shook her head.

"I like you Coop but I'm not the type of person that puts other women down or go after what obviously belongs to someone else. Don't let my music and persona fool you. I've been a follower of Zee Rose for years. She's an amazing woman Cooper. Anyway, I have to get going. Sometime us women want to know that our men are willing to fight for us. She didn't abandon you."

Cooper froze in place then turned his attention to Queen. "What did you just say?"

"I said, she didn't abandon you. I bet she's been waiting for you." Queen smiled and blew him a kiss before she sashayed out of his studio with her security and entourage in tow.

She didn't abandon him. That statement felt like a slap to the face; the kind only a mother could give. If he was honest with himself, he'd been letting his heart harden towards Zolee because he felt that she had abandoned him just like his biological family did. She had every right to be upset and with her history he should have been more understanding. Cooper lifted his phone and made his way to Zolee's IG page. He'd missed her so much. His days were not the same when he didn't talk to her or hear her obnoxious laugh over the phone. Zolee gave him life; he couldn't breathe without her. He loved the way she found joy in the smallest things, the fact that she was a health nut that couldn't stop eating bacon and the way she sighed whenever they embraced. Cooper even missed the fact that she loved to order something different so she could eat off of both of their plates when they ate out. He liked a few pictures then viewed her latest video. The camera loved her; she was a natural. When the clip finished, he smirked as he typed in a comment and hit send. *Can't wait to taste...*

Cooper entered the bar and looked around before he spotted his cousin. Deacon was sitting at a tall table and sipping on what could only be some expensive whiskey. That was his thing. Zolee was a whisky girl, something else he loved about her. It was rare to find a girl who could appreciate good alcohol when it didn't come in a fancy glass. Deacon spotted him and waved him over. He stood and hugged Cooper then patted him on the back.

"Damn little cuz! Long time no see."

"What do you mean? We saw each other on Thanksgiving."

"True, but I haven't heard from you since."

"Yeah shit has been busy. I haven't had time to do much of anything."

"Oh yeah? I heard that you have enough time to split between auntie, unc, and that Zolee chick."

Cooper couldn't hide the grin that was plastered on his face but he couldn't help it. Just hearing her name made him smile but it also made him feel like someone was squeezing the hell out of his heart.

"Aww, don't tell me that you're jealous."

"Nigga whateva." Deacon was more like a brother to Cooper. He grew up in a rough neighborhood and his mom begged his parents to take him in before he got himself killed. She had gotten wind that he was one of three masked men who had robbed a gas station. Two of them were caught but lucky for him they refused to snitch. Having a father figure changed Deacon's life. He graduated high school with honors and went on to graduate from Morehouse College. He used his business knowledge to run a successful real estate company. Him and his partners flipped houses, but he also had his hand in other businesses. If Deacon couldn't do anything else, he knew how to make money; he was a hustler. He even helped Cooper invest his money in some lucrative stock.

"So what's good Dee?"

"Same old shit. Work hard, play harder. I'm working on opening a restaurant and I need a partner." Deacon looked up at Coop in anticipation of his response to his not so subtle hint.

"Man you don't need a partner but if you're asking then I'm in."

"You're in? You haven't even heard my vision and seen the business plan."

"Nah, I don't need to." Cooper shook his head and ordered what Deacon was having when the waitress interrupted. "I know you, so I know that you put a lot of thought in this. You don't bring me in the mix if the risk is too high so I'm in. Let's do this."

"Bet but we'll talk about this in more detail when alcohol ain't involved."

Cooper and Deacon sipped their drinks while they bopped to the music and scarfed down wings and curly fries. Cooper eyed Deacon with suspicion. His cousin always had something to say, more specifically stories about his escapades with the ladies.

"Spit it out."

"Yo pretty ass just gon' sit here and not tell me that you haven't spoken to your girl since Thanksgiving?"

"It's times like this that I hate that you and mom are so close."

"Don't do us like that. She was worried about you and her. Auntie didn't like the state that she was in the night before y'all went to see the woman who shall remain nameless."

"What are you talking about?" Cooper sat up straight and gave Deacon his undivided attention.

"Well your mom found her in your room on the verge of a break down. The girl was in tears and sitting in front of her suitcase."

"Fuck maaannn. I had no idea that she was that upset. She woke up the next morning to go with me to meet my bio mom. Hell, she was up before me *and* she cussed her out!"

Even though Zo appeared to be strong and like she had it all together, Cooper couldn't forget her past and current struggles. There was a part of her that was still fragile. He should have handled her with better care and been more mindful of his reactions. Lashing out at Zo was the last thing he ever wanted to do and he never wanted her to see that side of him.

"Seriously? A real ride or die and she's in love with you. Sounds like a keeper."

"What? Love? Nah, it's too soon. Isn't it?"

"Aunt Lee seems to think so and I agree. There's no timeline on feelings Coop."

"And what about you, huh? I've never known you to be in a relationship. What's your deal?" Deacon wasn't fooled and knew that Coop was deflecting.

"Monogamy just ain't for me. That's all you Coop. I like being able to sample the many flavors of women without feeling like shit or having to explain myself to someone. The women I involve myself with have to understand there's no relationship and they ain't the only one."

"Is that why your roster consists of mostly married women?" Cooper raised an eyebrow.

"I didn't say I was a saint," Deacon replied with raised hands.

Cooper sat back in his seat and rubbed his chin. A group of women walked by and Deacon took his time to flirt with just a simple smile and checked each and every one of them out. Deacon was a ladies man and had no intentions of settling down. Deacon bringing up Zo put her in the forefront of Cooper's mind again. Whenever he thought of her he thought about the future. He knew in his gut that this thing with them wasn't supposed to end, not now and not after Valentine's day. Feelings had evolved and he couldn't let her go.

"I love her Deek."

Deacon's eyes shot over to Cooper in surprise. Although Cooper wanted love he'd never felt that the women he dated were deserving of it. He couldn't allow his vulnerability to be taken advantage of. With Zo, she pulled it out of him. She required that she be loved and that he let her in. It was in her actions, in the way she treated others. It made Cooper want to reciprocate ten times over which meant he needed to make sure he had a handle on his anger. He'd started back attending therapy weekly to sort through his issues and it was working. Deacon wiped his mouth and gave Cooper a look that said that he was down for whatever. Right or wrong, he always had Coop's back.

"Good for you. Now, what are you going to do about it?"

Winter

Chapter 10

Zolee paced the living area of her condo. They were supposed to be on their way to the Airbnb that they rented off the Gulf Coast to celebrate Christmas but Zolee ignored Ari's calls. She knew her girls were packing up the car and waiting on her. The sound of keys slapping against the door made Zolee spin around. Ari entered the apartment along with Ashli.

"Zo! What the hell? None of us like driving in the dark so we need to go now!"

"I can't, I'm not going. I'm not ready." The look of distress and pure fear on her face gave her friends pause.

"She's regressing." Ashli whispered to Ari. Ashli stood in Zolee's face, hands on her hips.

"You need to talk to him before he decides to move on."

"So, what! Let him move on. It wasn't supposed to be all of this any way. This was supposed to be fun, no strings attached. I need to get a hold on this." Zolee spoke animatedly with her hands.

"What are you going to do? Deny yourself of happiness? Shut your feelings off?"

"Yes! At least that way he won't hurt me." Tears trickle down her face. "I can't go through that hurt again. I am tired of fucking crying."

"Zo you can't give up on love because one jerk couldn't see how much of a blessing you were to him. Coop sees you; he recognizes your worth. Do you not notice the way he looks at you? Look I know what he said hurt your feelings. Ari and I get it. He wants to fix that, and you won't let him."

"He was just so angry that day. The look on his face. There was no emotion in his eyes. Almost like he wasn't there. Exactly like that night at the club. Remember?"

Ashli sighed and spoke in a softer tone. "Zolee, the Cooper you know today is so far removed from who he used to be. He used to be full of rage and for years none of the adults in his life could see it. He would stay quiet about a lot but would be boiling over in the inside, so he would take it out on bullies at school or in the neighborhood. It wasn't until he got arrested in college for fighting that he got help. It was self-defense but he almost killed the guy. The man ended up suffering from traumatic brain injury. Cooper still hasn't forgiven himself for that. He's so different with you Zo, but he's afraid of hurting you. It would break him to know that you're afraid of him."

"I'm not afraid of him!" Zolee snapped.

Ashli's head jerked back. She held up her finger and Ari knew this was about to go left. Ashli and Zo could fight like cats and dogs if you let them. Ari bumped Ashli out of the way and clutched Zolee's trembling hands.

"ZoZo, I know you. If you don't do this, then you will regret it. You must finish what you and Cooper started even if you decide to go your separate ways when you are done. The both of you are better for it."

"Yeah for real. He's been dying to lay eyes on you. It won't be awkward unless you make it that way."

"What if he shows up with someone else?"

Ashli and Ari looked at each other. Cooper called them almost every other day to get updates on Zo. Just yesterday he called Ashli five times to ask if she was coming. Ashli had to yell at him for him to chill out.

"Look, you got him wrapped around your finger. His ass ain't showing up with anyone. Coop is waiting on *you*. You had every right to be upset but he apologized and has done everything in his power to make it up to you. Got my best friend sending you new plants and crystals like you don't have enough already and you won't even answer his calls. Get your damn bag and let's go!"

Zolee crossed her arms and stared at them like a defiant child. She knew they were right but the fear of getting hurt was too crippling no matter how much she missed her friend. She missed his earthy manly scent, his smile and those deep dimples that went along with it. She missed his warmth and how he made her feel protected and secure. Zolee couldn't stop the tears from streaming down her face.

"Aww Zo."

"Here, eat the cookie!" Ashli pulled out a container out of her purse and peeled the top open. She didn't do well when her friends got emotional like this. Zolee frowned and shook her head.

"What? No. I don't want no damn..."

"Just eat the damn cookie!"

Zolee jumped and snatch a cookie and devoured it in two bites.

"Damn Zo. Slow down. I'm going to use the bathroom, but we are hitting the road when I get out."

Ashli took her time in the bathroom to give Zolee a minute to calm down. She just needed her to relax her mind and stop over thinking everything. Ashli stepped out of the bathroom while she applied lotion to her hands.

"Y'all ready?" The corners of Zolee's lips twitched before she grinned. Ari cut her eyes at Ashli.

"Yeah girl I was tripping. I'm starting to feel better now."

"Alright! Let's hit this road."

They were an hour away from their destination and Zolee was working on the second cookie that Ashli passed her.

"Mmm this cookie is so good. I can't wait to finally see Coop. I am going to ride his..."

"Hey! Okay, TMI. Ashli what was in those cookies?"

"Weed." Ashli shrugged before she bit into a cookie herself. Ari's eyes bucked.

"I cannot believe you Ashli Simone." Ashli raised her eyebrow.

"Oh, we using full names now? She'll be okay. She was at a ten and we needed her at four to get her in the car and endure the ride."

"Fine, but this is on you."

"Shh. Did you hear that?" Zolee broke out in a fit of laughter.

Ashli giggled and Ari rolled her eyes. It was going to be a long drive.

Another hour later they pulled up to the beach house they were renting for the holiday. The house was beautifully decorated with lights. By the looks of it they were the last to show up. Cooper and Deacon seemed to already be there.

"Thank God. I am starving!" Zolee hopped out of the car and waited for Ari to pop the trunk. They grabbed their respective luggage and Ashli led the way to the house. As soon as she entered Cooper was on her.

"Where the fuck have y'all been and why didn't anyone answer their phone? You were supposed to be here before us!"

Ashli and Zolee looked at each other and busted out laughing. Ashli brushed past him and headed straight for the kitchen. Cooper cut his eye at them then they accusatorily landed on Ari.

"Seriously?" His tongue moved over his teeth and his jaw clinched.

"Wait a minute. That was all your bestie right there. She drugged Zo with edibles to get her here."

"What the fuck? Ash has lost her damn mind," he growled.

"What's wrong?" Ari didn't understand why Cooper was so upset but it made her worry.

"Nothing, it's just that she... Nah, I can't. You have to talk to Zo about that. Ashli shouldn't have done that. That's not fuckin' cool. Come on ZoZo baby we got pizza in the kitchen." Cooper grabbed Zolee who couldn't stop laughing and led her to the kitchen to get her fed. Ari bent down to get her bags, but the rumble of a deep sexy voice stopped her.

"I'll get that for you lil' mama."

The man in front of her was gorgeous. He was tall, slim built, and looked like he was dipped in dark chocolate. He looked like pure sin and he oozed sex. When he smiled, he showed off a set of perfect white teeth.

"Um. I got it. Thank you." Dark chocolate had a grip on Ari's bag and wouldn't let loose.

"Come on now. That's not how we do things. Coop and I will take the bags up. I'm guessing you're Zolee's friend Ari. I'm Deacon."

"Yes, I'm Ari. Nice to meet you Deacon and thank you." Ari extended her hand, but Deacon simply looked at it and scoffed.

"Pick your room and I'll drop off your bags." Ari rolled her eyes and headed upstairs with Deacon behind her. Deacon couldn't help but grin as he walked in time of the sway of Ari's full and shapely hips.

In the kitchen Cooper was trying to remain calm but Ashli and Zo's antics caused his resolve to slowly unravel. After Ashli tried to pour both of them a third shot, he snatched the bottle from her hand.

"What got your panties in a bunch?"

"I'm not playing with you Ash. Stop! You two have had enough for tonight. Come on Zo, let's get you to bed." Cooper went to help Zolee off the stool. She snatched her arm from him so violently that Cooper had to catch her from stumbling backwards.

"You don't get to tell me what I've had enough of Coo-per. You're not my damn daddy! He's not here remember?" The kitchen fell silent. Zolee covered her mouth with her hands and gasped. Tears filled her eyes and it wasn't until she blinked that they fell down her cheeks.

"Baby..." Cooper slowly approached her but Zolee held her hands out.

"No! I'm fine. I just need to find my room and sleep." Ashli was quickly at Zolee's side to assist. She felt responsible for her current state and mouthed her apologies to Coop. Cooper instructed her on where to take Zolee before they headed up the stairs. After Ari came down to grab something to eat Cooper worked on putting everything up. When they arrived and realized the girls hadn't made it, him and Deacon went ahead and made a trip to a grocery store nearby to stock up the house. They would need to go back to get what they needed for Christmas Eve and Christmas.

As Ari was heading out of the kitchen Deacon sauntered in. He leaned over the counter and plucked a grape out of the fruit bowl. His eyes remained on Ari as she scurried out with her head down. Cooper eyes him pointedly.

"Don't even think about it Deek. Leave that one alone. Ari is Zolee's friend and I do not need you running through her and breaking her heart."

"We are all grown Coop. What's her story?" Cooper glared at Deacon then shook his head.

"Long-time boyfriend moved to Europe and was engaged to someone else months later."

"Damn. So, what's wrong with her?" Cooper shrugged and turned his mouth down.

"I mean she seems cool to me. They are definitely birds of a feather, but they all have their individual differences. Ari is the extrovert, knows how to have fun, a big people person, and she's the professional of the group. She's a therapist. I think she's the glue in their trio. Ashli and Ari had always remained close and she and Zo got close again this year. They no longer reach out for just holidays or birthdays."

Deacon nodded. "So, are you ready to make this official with ya girl?"

"Come on. You know I ain't never been afraid of commitment. I just didn't want to push things in a direction that she wasn't ready to go in, that *we* weren't ready to go in. This whole thing started off as something fun to do. At the time we both needed to experience something on a noncomplicated, no strings attached tip."

That was the goal but somehow things had gotten complicated and Cooper was positive that it was because they both had caught feelings and hadn't been honest about it. He goes through bouts of insomnia for weeks after they part ways. Zolee gave Cooper a sense of peace that he couldn't comprehend.

"So, when did things start to get complicated?"

"Right after Sasha's ass popped up in July. Zo was hot. Wanted to know if I was fuckin anyone and everything. Then she told me that she didn't want me with anyone else which I didn't argue because I wanted to knock a bitch out whenever I thought about her with anyone else."

"She was seeing other people?"

"Well one clown. I was a lame, but they were fucking I know that shit."

"Damn."

"That's Zo and that's why I need to lock her little ass down. She won't wait for me to fix it."

After having a nightcap with Deacon, Cooper was finally able to shower and get some rest. When he entered the bedroom, he was greeted with the soft sound of Zolee breathing and the light of the moon shining over her. She slept like she didn't have a care in the world. Cooper stood and watched her sleep until he started to feel like a creep. He went in the bathroom to wash up then situated himself on the other side of the bed. His arms itched to have Zo securely wrapped in them, but he fought the urge.

The warmth of the sun on her face made Zolee smile before her eyes could open. She could faintly hear the crashing waves from the ocean. Then she took a deep breath and froze. The clean sporty scent assaulted her senses and her eyes bucked open. Zolee shot up from the bed and shoved the warm body next to her until he stirred.

"Coop? Cooper wake up!"

"Huh? Man, Zo stop. Go on and do your meditation, yoga shit and let me sleep."

"I'm not playing with you Cooper. What are you doing in here?"

Cooper cursed under his breath before rolling over and facing her. Time seemed to stand still when they locked eyes. This was the closest they'd been since the last time they saw each other. Zolee was too faded to appreciate his presence the night before. She shook off the emotions that overtook her and suck her teeth.

"What are you doing in the bed with me?"

"What does it look like Zolee? I'm sleeping, well was sleeping."

"But I, we haven't... I haven't spoken to you since Thanksgiving."

"Zoe we're grown. I know what you taste like for crying out

110

loud. We all rented this place knowing that you and I were sharing a room."

Zolee blinked and Cooper was closer to her. She had no idea when it happened. Her breathing hitched when his fingers softly grazed her thigh.

"You don't want to share a bed with me Zo?" Cooper couldn't take his eyes off Zolee's lips as he licked his own. Zolee fidgeted under the covers before she jumped up out of the bed.

"Um I got to pee!"

Zolee slammed the bathroom door and locked it. She dragged her way to the sink and faced herself in the mirror.

"Get your shit together Zolee," she hissed. She took her time brushing her teeth and going through her skin care routine since someone had already placed her things on the sink. She untied her satin scarf and shook her locs free. When Zolee walked back into the room Cooper brushed past her and entered to bathroom without a word. Zolee went to her suitcase and pulled out a pair of gray leggings with a matching top. She slipped on a pair of colorful striped comfy socks. Zolee could smell the beginnings of breakfast downstairs and knew it was Ari. She was a great cook and had been working with Zolee on a food blog that they created content for on the weekends. Zolee busied herself with texting her mom and scrolling through Instagram, anything to keep her mind off Coop, his smile, his scent, his body. Zolee sat in the middle of the bed to meditate. She needed to center herself and calm the thoughts in her head. She needed a clear mind. After grounding herself Zolee slowly opened her eyes to Cooper standing over the bed watching her.

"Damn you really go somewhere else when you do that. I been moving around in here for ten minutes and you didn't flinch."

"Yeah I kind of do go somewhere else." Zolee's shoulders relaxed and she smiled.

"You ready to talk now?" Cooper pulled Zolee to the edge of the bed by her legs and she giggled and nodded her head. She had to admit to herself that she was tired of fighting; she didn't want to be angry at Coop. They sat shoulder to shoulder in silence. Cooper was the first to speak.

"I apologize for what I said to you and how I spoke to you at that rehearsal. I was dead ass wrong. Young Troy was flirting with you and that pissed me off. He was making you laugh, and I didn't know how to handle that. I let my anger get the best of me. It was never my intentions to take it out on you. That's not me and I don't ever want to treat you that way. I've struggled with my anger since I was a kid. I used to think being able to contain my anger meant that I had a handle over it, but it only made it worse. I've been going to counseling and learning ways to recognize my triggers and work through my anger. I don't want to snap at the people that I love. Please forgive me Zo."

"Cooper, I knew Young Troy wasn't shit. He wasn't fooling anybody. I was just playing nice for the kids. What *you* said was a trigger for me, but I had to realize that when you said those words to me, I wasn't seeing you I was seeing my ex. I was afraid of you leaving me like he did, but you're not him..." Zolee's words faded as she processed everything that Cooper said.

"Wait. You said that you didn't want to snap at the people that you love. Am I...?" Cooper's hand caressed her face. He leaned in so close that his lips brushed against hers when he spoke.

"I love you Zolee." Zolee leaned back, covered her mouth and gasped but the twinkle in her eye was not missed. Cooper grinned and tugged her hands down and replace them with his lips, pressing them into hers repeatedly. As they kissed Cooper licked around her pouty lips then sucked on her bottom lip. Zolee moaned into his mouth. Her skin tingled with anticipation. Cooper pulled Zolee onto his lap and she straddled him. Her tongue slipped into his mouth and Cooper eagerly sucked on it. She loved when he did that. Cooper always kissed her with wet passionate kisses. Cooper's hands splayed across her back and their tongues danced around each other to a rhythm they created. Zolee felt Cooper's hardness through his sweatpants. She smirked and pushed her hands past the band of his pants until she had him in her hands. Cooper growled and nipped at her neck.

"Zo! Get your ass up! Oh shit. Well damn... Go Zo!"

Shocked from Ashli's intrusion, Zolee jumped and attempted to stand up but Cooper held her in place. He continued planting kisses on her neck and shoulders.

"Coop," Zolee whispered and moaned.

"Get out Ash." Cooper grunted without looking up. Ashli rolled her eyes and slammed the door. She spoke from the other side.

"Y'all can do that shit later man. We have plans!" Zolee laughed through her embarrassment. She leaned back and stared into Cooper's eyes that were heavy with desire.

"I love you Coop." Cooper grinned. His piercing eyes roamed over her face and body. Cooper slowly licked up the side of her neck then tugged at her ear with his teeth pulling a groan out of her.

"Yeah I know. Now take your clothes off."

An hour later Cooper and Zolee finally made their way downstairs to smirks and coughs.

"Good morning?" Zolee looked around the room. Cooper grabbed a plate and started piling on food. Deacon looked at Ashli and Ari and smirked. When Cooper placed the plate in front of Zolee and kissed her on the forehead, Deacon's face fell. He pulled out two twenty-dollar bills and handed one to each of them. Ari took a sip of her mimosa.

"Told ya. I know my girl."

"What is going on?" Zolee addressed the room. "Did y'all bet on us?"

"Sure did. We bet Deek that *you* would put it on Coop." Ashli replied while waving the crisp bill at Deacon.

Zolee went and poured two glasses of mimosas and twisted her mouth up. She tilted her head to the side as she gave it thought.

"And how would you guys know if that was the case?" Cooper looked at Zolee in disbelief and she mouthed, *what?*

"He would come down here and fix your plate." The trio snickered as Coop choked on his food. He sipped from the bottle of water that he grabbed.

"Man, y'all can kiss my ass. At least I got someone to put it on me."

"That's right baby." Zolee sat next to Cooper and massaged the back of his neck.

Ashli pecked Cooper on the cheek. "Y'all are cute and I am glad that you two worked this out. Now we don't have to worry about this trip being awkward. Oh, and Zo I'm sorry about not telling you about the cookies. Coop was ready to take my head off."

"I accept. We're cool. Just give a heads-up next time." Zolee smiled and winked at Ashli. Just as Ari was getting up, she found herself face to face with Deacon who was heading towards the sink. They shared an awkward moment that didn't go unnoticed by Zolee. Her eyes lit up at the possibilities. Ari had every intention to see other people when Brandon moved but she hadn't been on a date after learning of his engagement. In fact, she'd thrown herself into her work. Ari cleared her throat and turned away from Deacon.

"Umm, good; now hurry up so we can go shopping."

Zolee and the girls found a local outlet mall where they finished up their Christmas shopping. Zolee hadn't expected Coop to really show up so she left the gift that she'd had for him at home. He was a sneaker head, so she snagged him a pair of the Air Jordan Dub Zeros in all black. She couldn't wait to see the look on his face when he unwrapped them. Zolee teased Coop on his shoe addiction so it would be an unexpected gift. They were now on their way back home to relax and freshen up before heading out for dinner.

"Zo, can I ask you something?" Ari broke into Zolee's thoughts.

"Hmm? Yeah, of course. What's up?"

"When Cooper found out about Ashli getting you high and drunk, he was beyond pissed. The man was breathing fire. It was apparent that he fought hard not to go off on us but when I tried to question it, he said that I needed to talk to you. What did he mean by that?"

Zolee sighed and dropped her head. Her palms rubbed against her thighs. Ari who was driving, glanced over then caught Ashli's concerned expression in the rearview mirror.

"Zo, you can trust us." Zolee knew without a doubt that she could trust her friends, but she didn't want them to worry. She didn't need them making a fuss out of this. She also didn't want them to think that she needed to be handled with kid gloves. Zolee was strong and she would not allow herself to fall that deep again. For the first time in a long time she felt whole and absolutely free.

"Promise you guys won't freak out." When neither of them responded she spoke firmer. "Promise me, please."

"We promise ZoZo. You've been hiding a part of you since Mr. Norwood passed away. Ash and I are your friends. You can unload on us."

Zolee didn't speak right away, instead she turned her attention towards the window as Ari drove. Soulful Christmas music played on the radio and Ashli sat in the backseat singing along, off key. Ari tapped the steering wheel and hummed. They were both growing impatient with her stalling.

"Um, after my dad died, I hit a really rough patch and it only worsen when my mom started to date Charlie. My drinking got out of control and I was smoking weed heavily. I needed both to get through the day. Wake and bake in the morning and drank until I passed out at night. When I started having thoughts of ending my life, so I sought help. That's why I don't drink like I use to and I hadn't smoked since I started therapy over a year ago."

"Shit Zo, I am so sorry. I didn't know." Ashli's voice cracked. Her hand rested on Zolee's shoulder and she gave a gentle squeeze.

"I knew something was wrong. I should have said something. I *knew* better." Ari patted the tears that ran down her face and sniffled. She reached for Zolee's hand. "If you ever find yourself in that place again I need you to tell us. Don't do that again."

"I won't. At the time I didn't want to worry anyone, and I didn't think it was that serious until it was almost too late. I'm learning to recognize the signs so that I can seek comfort and help."

"The Christmas holiday has previously been hard for you. How are you managing?" Ari questioned.

"I am actually doing surprisingly good. I'm able to acknowledge when I am sad and work through it but it's not consuming me like it has for the last three years. When I think about dad now, I can remember the good and actually smile."

"That's great. We want nothing more than for you to find your joy again. I think you have." Ari smirked; her focus remained on the road as she followed the navigation on the SUV.

Zolee only nodded then bobbed her head to the music from the radio.

"He told me that he loved me." Zolee smiled at the memory.

"What?" Both Ashli and Ari yelled in unison.

"Yep! Last night." Zolee replayed the moment in her head. She wrapped her arms around herself and dreamily looked out the passenger window.

"Bitch you better have told him you love him too!" Ashli yelled and pushed the back of the seat. Zolee jerked forward and laughed.

"Heffa, don't make me climb back there. Of course, I did. Damn I never thought that I would have this feeling again. It's different though. I thought what Lo and I had was love, but it wasn't, not like that. How I felt about him doesn't come close to what I feel for Coop." Zolee looked back at Ashli and beamed, then she turned to Ari and gave her the same look.

"This chick is glowing. It's a good look boo and Cooper needs a normal woman who ain't hungry for attention and fame. He has a little edge to him, but Coop is simply a good guy at the end of the day. I could not stand Sasha. She was a low class opportunistic..."

"Bitch." Zolee finished her sentence.

"Yeah Cooper told me about y'all run in and how it bothered him not to know exactly what transpired between the two of you."

"Not much to tell. It was more of how our interaction made me feel. I was jealous and in that short moment realized that the thought of Cooper sharing a part of him intimately with anyone else made me want to drag both Sasha and Coop. The both of you know that I am far from insecure, but I felt it in that moment, and I took it out on Coop. It was totally out of character for me, but he pulled that out of me."

"Well you're going to have to reel that in friend because Cooper is sort of like a celebrity in his own right. He has a huge following and the ladies want him. He's like some sort of sex symbol with his annoying ass."

"Yeah I hear you but he's also going to have to tame that temper when it comes to other men and me."

"I have a nagging feeling that it will never be a dull moment with the two of you." Ari regarded Zolee as she pulled up to the house.

"Yeah because they are both moody and aggy as hell!"

Zolee was over the moon about patching things up with Cooper and being honest about their feelings but she was unsure of what would happen come February. Although they said they loved each other they hadn't talked about whether they would continue this journey at the end of their year together. She prayed that it wouldn't come to an end.

Pecks from soft lips pressed into Zolee's skin and set fire to her lips, neck, and breast. She hissed when teeth tugged at her taunt nipple then his wet tongue swirled and sucked to take away the sting. Zolee smiled then groaned.

"Coop?"

"Wake up beautiful. It's Christmas."

There were white lights twinkling on the ceiling and the room smelled like pine and cinnamon sugar cookies.

"What time is it Coop?"

"Four in the morning. I wanted you all to myself before the house wakes up." He flashed her that sexy boyish grin that made Zolee want to give him whatever he wanted. She couldn't deny him if she wanted to. Zolee whined as she sat up in the bed and tugged her scarf off.

Cooper sat at the foot of the bed and took in Zolee's beauty. Her wild locs had grown almost past her breast and she was topless; the white covers pooled around her waist. She looked like an angelic seductress. Zolee was dangerous and brought feelings out of

Cooper that he'd never felt romantically. He would love and protect this woman at all cost. It was now his responsibility to keep a smile on her face. She didn't blink once under his watchful eye, instead she bit her bottom lip and moan; she was turned on. *That damn Zolee.*

"Merry Christmas," she whispered. Zolee shook her head and grinned. "Can you believe I haven't said that since before daddy?"

"Merry Christmas Zo baby. How do you feel?"

"Hopeful, happy; like me. I feel blessed Coop. There were so many lonely nights when I laid in bed and prayed for this day. I can breathe again, and you played a pivotal role in that. Looking back on how this year played out you were the answers to my prayers." Zolee still spoke barely above a whisper but it was so quiet that Cooper had no trouble hearing her. He crawled next to her and handed her a small box and a large box, both beautifully wrapped. Zolee's eyes lit up and she smiled so big her eyes looked closed.

"Who wrapped these for you?"

"My mom." Cooper shrugged. "Open the small box first."

Zolee eagerly ripped at the paper with childhood glee. It was then that she realized that it was most likely jewelry in the velvet box. Inside were a set of diamond studs and small silver hoops. The flawless diamonds sparkled under the lights. Zolee gasped and covered her mouth with her small hand.

"Oh Coop. You didn't…"

"I did. Your dad was exposing you to how you should be treated and the things that you deserved. If diamonds don't do it for you, then I will get you whatever your heart desires. Are we clear on that?"

"Yes. They are beautiful. I love it. Thank you." Zolee leaned into kiss Cooper and he gave her a quick peck on the lips. She pouted.

"Slow your roll with your fast ass. You have one more gift to open." Cooper sat the large gift on her lap and she took her time opening this one as she kept stealing glances at Cooper. It was a large frame that had smaller frames for individual pictures. The best part about it was that the frame was already filled with pictures; pictures that highlighted the awesome year that she had. There were pictures from the Valentine's party; someone had snuck a few candid photos and caught her and Cooper's first interactions. He included pictures from the holidays they spent together. There was a specific one from the Fourth of July with Zolee dancing with the sparklers. It showed her silhouette so no one would be able to tell that she was naked. Zolee laughed and blinked away tears. These tears felt different; they were tears of joy.

"I can't believe you did this."

"So, you like it?" Cooper caressed her face then kissed her nose.

"I love it." What she loved most about it was the thought he put into the gift. Lorenz use to buy her lavish gifts but most of them weren't even her style. Cooper knew that as a photographer Zolee would love the frame filled with cherished memories. They were a reminder of her rebirth, her growth.

"Um I left your original gift at home, but I was able to find you something when we went shopping."

"Your forgiveness was all I wanted for Christmas Zo but thanks for the shoes. They're dope." Cooper smirked.

"Coop! You opened your gift already? I can't believe you." Zolee punched him in the arm and he tossed her head back and laughed. "Big ass kid."

"Yo! I could tell it was a shoe box and I couldn't help it."

"Let's make this our tradition."

"What?"

"Opening our gifts for each other alone; just the two of us. It feels good." Cooper smirked and moved the gifts off the bed and placed them on the dresser.

"As long as we add one more thing to that tradition."

"And what's that?"

"I follow up with giving you multiple orgasms." Before Zolee could respond Cooper had dipped under the covers and his warm tongue flatten against her center. Zolee head fell back and she pushed her pelvis into Cooper's skillful tongue.

"Mmm Coop. Dammit! Merry Christmas baby."

Christmas was perfect, better than Zolee could imagine. The

only thing that was missing was her mom and Charlie. They chatted on FaceTime before dinner and her mother panned in on her gifts under the tree. All of her friends had gifts including Cooper. The plan was to spend New Year's Eve back in Miami partying it up. They'd gotten tickets to Club Liv that included free champagne and tapas all night. Zora couldn't hide her excitement when Zolee shared that she'd forgiven Coop and showed her the gifts including the picture frames they both gifted each other. To her surprise Ari snatched up Cooper's gift before they left the house and even wrapped it for her. It turned out that she and Cooper had similar ideas. Zolee wanted Cooper to have something to remind him of the love that surrounds him daily. His frame included pictures of Ashli, his students, his family on Thanksgiving and photos of him and her. Her heart swelled at the memory of Cooper's reaction. He'd choked up in front of the whole gang.

"Everyone in this frame are people who love you. People who will always be with you, unconditionally."

"Shit Zo, this is… this is… Damn I couldn't have asked for a better gift." A single tear escaped, and Cooper quickly brushed it away. Zolee blinked away her own tears, grabbed him by the face and kissed him. They kissed like they were the only two in the room until Deacon's voice broke through.

"Happy the two of you made up and all but where are my gifts?"

The rest of the evening was spent eating and playing games. Zolee picked up a little chemistry between Ari and Deacon but Cooper told her to stay out of it. She wouldn't say anything to Deacon, but she would definitely have a chat with Ari when they got back home. That night, after everyone had gone to their rooms or somewhere to be alone Zolee lay peacefully in the bed as Coop held her from behind and massaged her scalp. She relaxed in his strong arms and his minty breath caressed the back of her neck and shoulders. He told her that he slept better with her in the bed with him.

Secured in his arms Zolee realized that what she and Lo had wasn't true love. Lo had a wandering eye from the day they met, and she made the decision to ignore it. The friendship was real and they had love for each other, but they had no business engaging in a relationship. They stayed together out of comfort. What she felt with Cooper was raw, unnerving, yet exhilarating. Cooper saw Zolee and she saw him. They couldn't hide their feelings from each other. It felt good to be seen.

"Zo." His deep sensual voice made her shiver. She heard a light chuckle; he knew the effect that he had on her. Zolee placed a couple of kisses on his arm.

"Yes?"

"Take your ass to bed." Zolee smiled then drifted off to sleep.

Chapter 11

Cooper nervously maneuvered around the kitchen in preparation for the night. He wanted everything to be perfect; she deserved it. His mom walked him through making lasagna with homemade garlic bread on FaceTime while his dad cracked jokes. He made the salad by himself which pretty much consisted of him pouring it out of the bag and adding tomatoes, red onions, cucumbers, and banana peppers. After the lasagna was in the oven, he cleaned the kitchen, then washed up and changed clothes. Zolee should be knocking soon, he thought to himself. Cooper had rented the penthouse suite at the Fontainebleau, a Christmas gift from Queen.

There was a light tap on the door and Cooper came out of the bedroom while he buttoned up his shirt. His heart was beating fast, so he took a few deep breaths before he pulled the door open. Zolee stood on the other side looking ravishing. She was wearing an emerald green strapless mini that hugged all of her curves. Her locs were in some type of intricate up do; her skin was glowing. They both shamelessly checked each other out from head to toe. Their smiles revealed that they were both pleased.

"Zo."

"Coop."

"Get in here."

Cooper grabbed Zolee's delicate hand and pulled her into the suite. Zolee's attention immediately went straight to the windows and the Miami skyline; it was beautiful.

"Wow! This is nice and it smells so good. What did you cook?"

"Lasagna. Matter of fact..." Cooper quickly spun around and jogged to the kitchen. He pulled the lasagna out of the oven and cursed under his breath. Another few minutes and he would have burned dinner. The cheese was a little browner than he wanted it, but at least the meal would be edible.

"Mmmm. You cooked this?" Zolee leaned over his shoulder and stepped back so that he could pull it out of the oven.

"What you think?"

"Okay I see you. I must be pretty special for you to want to cook."

"You are." Cooper stared at her with so much intensity that Zolee diverted her eyes, but Cooper was on her in seconds, tilting her chin back up and devouring her mouth. His kisses were urgent and passionate. He had her head spinning. Zolee was tempted to slip out of her dress and drop to her knees. Cooper had her open like 7-Eleven.

"Let's eat," he whispered in her ear. He made her sit at the table while he brought out the food and wine. They ate in silence with the occasional moans or "Oh my God" from Zolee. Cooper was entranced by her; he loved watching her eat. Zolee made eating look so damn hot. Cooper didn't have much of an appetite, so he sipped his wine and enjoyed her taking pleasure in eating his food.

"This was great Coop. I can't believe you did all of this for me."

"You deserve it baby. I just wanted to make today special."

"Are you okay? You've been more quiet than usual, and you barely touched your food."

"Nah, I'm good. Just got some shit on my mind." Cooper rubbed his sweaty palms on his pants before he stood up and cleared off the table. Zolee stood to help.

"I got it Zo!" He was on edge.

"Coop." Zolee looked like she was ready to pop off. She could have stayed home if the night was going to take a turn for the worse.

"That came out wrong. Let me handle this, you have another glass of wine and turn on some music. My playlist is already set up just hit play." Cooper smiled but his eyes wouldn't connect with hers.

Zolee nodded and made her way over to his phone near the sound system. She wondered what had changed in the time between her walking into the suite and dinner. Cooper was acting strange and it was making her anxious. She thought the night would end differently but now she was back wondering if he'd planned on going through with ending things tonight. Maybe he'd changed his mind and was struggling to find the words. *Why do all of this? Why not just keep it simple?* She thought to herself. Jill Scott, *He Loves Me* played as she stared into the night sky. On the beach she could see the waves crashing and some weird flickering lights on the sand. She narrowed her eyes to focus on what the lights could possibly be.

"Baby come check out this view." Cooper stood with the door open and that sexy, dimpled lopsided smirked that Zolee adored. She didn't even hear him walk up on her. Her eyes lit up and she allowed Cooper to lead her outside. They were greeted with a gentle breeze and the smell of saltwater.

"Is it too cool for you?" Cooper cleared his throat and rubbed his hands up and down her arms.

"Um a little."

Cooper released her and walked the length of the balcony to turn on the heated lamps. Zolee leaned over the railing and took in the view. She smiled when she smelled his intoxicating cologne. Coop held her from behind and kissed the top of her head. His heart was pounding fast and strong; her heartbeat followed the same cadence.

"Are you happy Zo?" His breath caressed her neck as he spoke, then his soft lips pressed into her cheek. Her body was instantly warmed up.

"Yes, anytime that I'm with you. I can't believe that it's already been a year. That means... Thank you Coop. This last year has been unforgettable, and I owe a part of that to you. Thank you for everything." She held on tightly to his bicep.

"It doesn't have to end here Zo. What happened to all that talk about our Christmas tradition?" He turned their bodies so that they could face each other.

Zolee shook her head and let it drop. Her hands gripped his shirt. "Coop." He tilted her chin back up.

"I wasn't playing when I said that I loved you Zo and that's not something that I can shut off just because I completed my promise to you. Check it. How about I make another promise?"

Zolee's eyes questioned him. She was nervous and unsure of what he was about to say. When she stared at him, she couldn't imagine her life without him in it. He was a part of her tribe now. She nodded her head and his lips pressed into hers.

"I promise to bring more laughs than tears. I promise to protect you. I promise to be your best friend. I promise to cherish and respect you and our relationship." He bit his bottom lip and grinned. "I promise you days and nights of mind-blowing sex. I promise to always provide for you and support your dreams. I promise to love you forever and be the best husband I can be, if you would have me." Cooper's eyes filled with unshed tears while Zolee allowed her tears to fall.

"What are you...?" Cooper motioned for her to look back down on the beach. The strange flickering lights formed into words. *Will you marry me?* Zolee's hands shot to her mouth and she gasped. As tears continued to stream down her face, she turned to Cooper who was down on one knee holding up the most perfect chocolate diamond ring in a rose gold setting.

"I can't go another day without making you mine. Zolee Rose Norwood, will you marry me?"

Zolee eagerly shook her head. "Yes. Yes, yes, yes!" She punctuated each yes with a kiss. Cooper's hand trembled as he slipped jaw dropping ring on her finger.

"What the fuck Cooper?"

"Zo."

"Sorry but... this ring! Are we really doing this?"

"It looks like it ZoZo baby. Are you seriously ready to be Mrs. Powers?"

"Of course; as soon as possible." Zolee swayed to the music. She held her hand out and stared at her ring.

"What about in a week?"

"Huh, what? Seriously? My mom would kill me." Zolee stopped in her tracks and looked up at him. Her eyes sparkled with excitement and mischief. "Let's do it." Cooper's mouth crashed into Zolee's and she climbed up his body and wrapped her arms and legs around him; he walked them back into the house towards the bedroom.

"Happy Valentine's Day Zo."

"Happy Anniversary Coop."

The End

Connect with TaKisha Trenean

Facebook: @takishatrenean

Instagram: @takisha_trenean

Amazon: amazon.com/author/takishatrenean

About The Author

Takisha Trenean

Born and raised in Miami, Florida, TaKisha Trenean is both a writer and an avid reader. TaKisha has always had a passion for writing and enjoys giving life to characters through penning stories. Throughout her formative years she would journaling and write poetry as a form expressing herself and documenting her experiences. TaKisha eventually began working on her first novel as a creative outlet to heal from a personal loss. Writing romance gives life to  the hopeless romantic within her and allows the introvert within to explore life through her characters. Using music and the world around her, TaKisha hopes to create stories that readers can ultimately relate to and get lost in.

Books By This Author

For The Love Of You: A Miami Street King Novel

For The Love Of You 2: A Miami Street King Novel

Love Will Never Do Without You

Kindred Hearts

Love Captured: A Sweet Sexy Savage Novel

Love Awakened: A Sweet Sexy Savage Novel

www.ingramcontent.com/pod-product-compliance
Lightning Source LLC
Chambersburg PA
CBHW021204130626
46554CB00005B/1986